LEEDS LIBRARIES

Revenge Riders

Hawk had Indian forebears, but lived the life of a peaceful rancher. Until, that is, the bandits came. With his wife dead and his son gone, kidnapped and beyond finding, Hawk returns to the ways of his people. He goes hunting, only this time he is hunting for the hardest game of all – the evil men who have committed the attack.

Along with the men who have worked for him for most of his life, Hawk finds out that a member of his wife's family has conspired against him, but who is the mysterious girl with his son? What is the connection between the kidnappers and the bandits?

As Hawk digs deeper he becomes the unwilling leader of men who need to track down the bandits who have devastated their once-peaceful community. A seemingly idealistic leader has taken hostage many people for his own evil purposes and Hawk must find out why.

Revenge Riders

Alex Frew

A Black Horse Western

ROBERT HALE

© Alex Frew 2019
First published in Great Britain 2019

ISBN 978-0-7198-3027-3

The Crowood Press
The Stable Block
Crowood Lane
Ramsbury
Marlborough
Wiltshire SN8 2HR

www.bhwesterns.com

Robert Hale is an imprint
of The Crowood Press

Typeset by
Derek Doyle & Associates, Shaw Heath
Printed and bound in Great Britain by
4Bind Ltd, Stevenage, SG1 2XT

CHAPTER ONE

Jay Hawk had come to terms with the bandits. Not actual speaking terms, just the kind of terms where he accepted that bandits lived and roamed in the area of Hatton Falls, Texas. This was pioneer country quite a few years after the Civil War. Like it did for so many others, the war stood out in his mind. He had been a boy at the time and was now a man in his early forties with a family of his own, but he remembered the struggles of that time well. Sometimes in the middle of the night, when he couldn't sleep and had to get up for a smoke, he thought back to those times. Although long gone, in the early hours they seemed like yesterday.

His father, a man much on his mind, had been a member of the Blackfoot Sioux and had acted as a scout for the blues during the war. Neither accepted by the people who employed him – because he was Indian – nor welcome once his job was done, Hawk senior had one factor in his favour; he had fallen in love with, and had married, one of the pioneer women when he himself was already in middle age. That woman had been Anna,

Hawk's mother, who was the daughter of a Scots Missionary who had brought his particular brand of Presbyterian religion out to the untracked wilderness of the so-called Wild West.

Hawk's father had brought his family out to Texas on the strength of his connections, and had been accepted as a part of the community in a way that many of the Indians had not. This did not mean that everyone had treated Hawk senior in a kind or favourable manner, but with his wife and her family behind him and a natural drive to get forward in life, Hawk senior had built up a life in these lands, before dying at the age of sixty. He'd left all his property, his land and his stock to his one surviving son some fifteen years before. Life out here on the plains of Texas was hard, but there was no other place Hawk would rather be. His own son Rye, short for Ryan, was sleeping in the other bedroom of their roomy, one level ranch. There was a faint smile of pride on his otherwise impassive features as he thought of the young man, eighteen years old and in full physical strength.

In the other bedroom was his wife. The smile vanished now that he could hear her breath rasping as he sat out here in the shaded back porch.

No one knew what the disease was. Some kind of lung infection that was sure, one that prevented her from drawing a deep breath when she wanted, a condition that made her weak and dizzy when she tried to stand, while getting worse all the time.

He drew on his hand-rolled cigarette and felt the tobacco soothe away some of the gremlins that proliferated inside his head. She was his Mary, from the same

6

kind of stock as his mother. A solid, dependable woman, but bright and attractive, who had made his heart sing in a way that no other could when they had married in their late teenage years, and it had been that way ever since, twenty-odd years later. He just did not want to live life without her: only the thought of his son keeping him going.

He had no more time to contemplate the inner workings of his life. A man called. Hawk rose and walked round the shadowy corner of the porch and the same man appeared at the front of the ranch, and nodded to Jay to come forward. Even from his outline Jay recognized Yancey Barnes, a big, solid man who, in contrast to Hawk's naturally slim build, was as thickset and wide as the very type of door after which he was named. It was said that at Thanksgiving in the village he was able to eat half a turkey, a big one, in one sitting. Some people considered him to be half-witted but he was strong and did as he was told, so he was always able to find employment in the ranches where hard labour was always needed to deal with the huge herds of cattle.

'Hoya,' said Yancey, a strange kind of greeting he employed with those he knew.

'What are you doing about here at this hour?' asked Hawk, a direct man.

'Strange things is happening,' said Yancey. 'Don't know a lot, so to speak, but there's been things happening around the ranches o' this district.' He was standing beside the main gate of the ranch and came forward with a look of concern on his face, just barely visible in the gathering light of the day. 'I know you come out here early at times. Can't sleep, I think.' He entered the shadow of an outhouse, a strange outline of a man despite his bulk, his voice barely raised above a whisper. Hawk, who had been meaning to get back to his bed for a couple of hours once he had soothed his nerves with a smoke, came forward to ask this unwanted pest to leave.

He did not have the chance to do this. A piece of the outbuilding turned out to be a shadowy figure that rushed at him from one side. He did not even have time to turn around before a thump on his head sent him to the ground, his last impression being the grateful thought that at least he did not have a hard path up to his property.

He awoke with the sun still low in the sky, a dry mouth and an aching head. Luckily his face was the shade of his father's so the sun had not burned his skin, although the day was heating up. He rose and staggered towards the ranch building, seeing at once that the door was hanging wide.

'Mary,' he said as he staggered inside, still fighting off the dizziness caused by the blow, 'Ryan, where are you?'

His wife gave a groan and he went into the bedroom. Her face and hands, the only bits he could see, were whiter than the coverlet beneath which she lay.

'Noises ... heard noises in the night ... been here, couldn't ... couldn't move. Rye, where is he? I heard noises.'

He left his wife and went into Ryan's bedroom. His son was gone. His first thought was that there was no sign of a struggle: the blankets were still intact, although thrown aside, and nothing had been knocked over except for the candle and dish that sat at the side of his bed ready to be lit. The books lined up on the shelf facing his bed – Shakespeare, the Bible, books on law (he was a smart boy), one or two dime novels – were lying in different directions as if the shelf had been banged, but apart from that there was nothing wrong with the room. Hawk, though, had extremely acute senses and he caught the acrid scent in the air of some chemical that he recognized – chloroform. It was a substance that was all the rage now with Texan doctors because it was easily stored in brown carboy bottles, and was a substance that could be used to knock a man out during a surgical procedure. The only reason he knew the scent was that the previous year he had been in an accident, a riding injury, and he had to have his broken leg set. The pain had been excruciating, and the local doctor had used the chemical for the first time. He had been grateful for the easing of the agony, but he would never forget that sweetish smell and the feeling of suffocation that followed its use.

He went back to the room where Mary lay in almost an attitude of prayer, one hand lightly sitting on top of another.

'Is he . . . is he all right?' she gasped, forcing the words out. He looked at her upturned face and he did what any merciful person would have done in the circumstances. He lied.

'Rye's fine,' he said, 'he just went out early to deal with some scattered longhorns we need to round up 'fore they get into rocky territory.'

'I heard noises . . . in the night. You weren't there.'

9

'Bad dreams is all they were, Mary.' He fought an impulse to take her in his arms and hold her tight, knowing that in her condition he would harm her fragile body. He stroked her brow and could see her taking comfort from his touch.

'Good,' she said, wanting to hear only things that soothed her. 'Tell him . . . Tell him I love him. It's time, Jay.'

'No,' he said, knowing what she meant. 'No, that can't be right. You're a fighter. You'll win this one too, you'll get better.' But he was a man mouthing words, and that was all they were.

She smiled suddenly, and her face lit up like that of the Mary he had known so long ago when they were young, setting out on the road of marriage with barely their parent's approval. 'You were a good husband. You're a good man. Look after Ryan.'

He was holding her hand by then, and as she sank back on the pillow after raising her head slightly, he heard a rattle in her throat that said more than any words, then she closed her eyes, that old familiar half smile on her lips, and died.

He sat there for a long time, thoughts rushing through his head of their life together, how she had worked tirelessly with him to build up the ranch that his father had left as his legacy. She had carried four children for him, only the youngest surviving, while none of the others had lived beyond four years. She had not been a wife; she had been far more than that. Too many wives were just a person who carried the children and stayed at home to cook for their rancher husbands. She had been far more than that; she had been his lifelong companion and his dearest friend. He had seen a parting in the long future, too far away to even think about, and now she was gone forever. He took hold of her and held her in his arms for a long time. The tears did not come, that was not his way, but he held her and was glad that he had helped her pass in peace with a lie about what had happened to her beloved son.

CHAPTER TWO

The fire was not a thing that seemed to be planned, but when it burned, the whole village of Hatton Falls was out to bring it to a halt. Like all villages they were situated near a river – a fork of the mighty Brazos – at a time of the summer when the waters were low and they had no hoses or horse-drawn fire wagons where the water could be pumped by hand through the hoses. Such things were only kept in places like Houston, and some of the bigger towns round about. The only water stored around here was in wooden barrels, gathered from the waters or the river or from the god of the sky. Worse still, the place that was on fire was the saloon, ironically called the Watering Hole.

Starting just before dawn, the fire was a focus for almost the entire population as they brought out every container they could think of and slung the contents at the thick flames that leapt from the foundations. They had a reason to be worried: Hatton was built from the plentiful wood that abounded in this county, and if the fire spread across the twenty or so buildings that constituted the small town it would take grip fast and hard in these dry conditions. Given that the population of the village was smaller than one hundred souls it was clearly in the interests of every man, woman and child to pull together.

It would be hard to think of an easier way to get everyone in one place, which was what the fire was for. Just as they had got it under control there was the sound of horses' hoofs, and every resident was confronted by the sight of what seemed like an endless stream of beasts coming down the one main street. They could see a variety of horses, and on them big solid Mexican bandits, all armed with a variety of weapons that would satisfy a small army – which is what they were.

The raiders wasted no time whatsoever. They dismounted from their big steeds and quickly took charge of the proceedings. They were dressed in traditional garments, most of them, wrapped in ponchos against the chill of the early morning air, grey woollen leggings and wide-brimmed straw hats. Their obvious leader was a tall, somewhat austere-looking man. Most of them had big moustaches of varying shapes and sizes, but he was clean-shaven and wore dark, almost military-type clothes. His black trousers were tucked into long riding boots and he was not slow to point out what was going to happen.

'People, all of you, you are coming with me and my men. There is no other way! Surrender now or die.'

This was not a place where people carried guns out of habit, but one of the men who had been fighting the fire, a big, bristling shopkeeper, pulled a pistol out of his deep pocket where he kept it all the time and ran forward, aiming it straight at the stranger's heart. In a long street with no escape bristling with weapons from every angle – because the horsemen had come in from every side – this was a foolish, not a brave thing to do. A whole host of weapons sounded at once and the air was thick with the smell of gunpowder before his finger even had time to squeeze the trigger. He fell forward on his face, the blood that poured from his body looking black in the early twilight. His wife, a big woman of uncertain age, rushed forward to his side and fell on to her knees sobbing.

Another woman, a young one this time, started running into the shadows, a ploy that might have worked, allowing her to hide in the darkness outside the village where the hills and woodlands mounted up rapidly, but she too was halted when a young Mexican stepped forward and smacked her on the side of her head with the butt of his rifle. She too fell to the ground and lay there sobbing, crying and screaming.

Stepping forward, the military-looking man engaged their attention and held up his arms. 'All of you,' he said in ringing tones, 'are going to be working for a greater purpose from now on. If you behave, you will be treated well. If not . . . well, you see what has already happened. I, Aguste Rivero, promise you this thing. Obey my men now.' The authority in his stance and his words seemed to draw all the fight out of the villagers. These were not military people: they were shopkeepers, the owner of a livery, a hardware store keeper and his family, and others of similar ilk. The so-called soldiers of the invaders soon tied the arms of the people, male, female, young and old

14

alike, and made them walk in procession, leaving the village on the earliest light of day, weaving their way through the woodlands and into a trail that led into the hills.

They had been enslaved.

Hawk should have gone in search of his son; he knew that. An obvious loss like that could not be followed by a wait to see what was going to happen. He was the son of an Indian scout, he knew the ways of the hills and he had a wide knowledge of the area.

The trouble was, his wife was lying dead in their – his – bedroom, and the heat of the day, combined with the time it took for decay to begin, meant that she would have to be buried soon, and not in the way he would have wanted. She would have desired a church service with all of her friends (and they were many) present, with most of the mourners there when she was interred. He was not going to miss the burial of the woman who had been with him for most of his adult life. He had to get help, he knew that much. At that moment he was still beside her, his Mary. He folded her hands over again and tenderly arranged her hair, then did the only thing he could under the circumstances: he went for his men.

The bunkhouse was situated only a few hundred feet from the ranch, but in such a way that it was on the other side of a bluff. Mary had liked it that way, had always wanted to keep her home life separate from the work they were doing. Hopefully some of his men would be back from their work. If he didn't appear to work with them, as sometimes happened because of the paperwork

15

that had to be done, they would quite happily go out and perform their duties on their own, experience giving them all the direction they needed.

The bunkhouse was a big building made of a mixture of adobe foundations and wooden walls, with a tiled, pitched roof that sloped down to keep off the sweeping winter rains. The building had been constructed in such a way that it could house twelve, or at a pinch, fourteen men. At this time of year – it was early summer – Hawk did not need that number, and employed only three full-time cowboys who would see to the needs of his cows and make sure that they didn't stray too far, especially when they were calving.

There was a frantic beat in the back of his mind telling him to go, to let whoever was there know that his wife was dead, so that they could bury her and he could just leave to find his son, but that wasn't going to be the way.

He expected only one of his men to be there, perhaps, since that was the usual way, but all three of them were there when he arrived: Alonzo Clay, Frank Flynn, and Logan Holt.

They were dressed pretty much alike in the blue canvas jeans that had become so popular lately, with waistcoats under their jackets. All three of them were sitting with their hats on, with various bits and pieces of equipment at their sides as they sat around an open fire in front of the bunkhouse, drinking steaming mugs of coffee.

'Hi, boss,' said Frank in his easy manner as Hawk appeared. 'Having a long lie in today?' He was being humorous, of course – no man worked longer hours in the business than his boss.

'My wife, my Mary, just died,' said Hawk. Six simple words, but they were enough.

The three men in front of him got to their feet and fell over themselves saying how sorry they were. They had all been expecting this news for some time, but even an expected death, when it happens, can cause surprise due to the circumstances. 'Finish your coffee,' said Hawk, 'and help me bury her.'

With the four working together the actual burial did not take that long. There was a spot at the back of the ranch that had long been reserved as a burial site. A lone yew tree with spreading branches and a gnarled trunk was the custodian of the area, which was surrounded by a low stone wall that Hawk's father had constructed with his own hands. There was room in the graveyard for more than twenty burials. His father was in there with a simple headstone to mark his grave. His mother's stone was there too, by the side of the first one, for she had died of a broken heart a year after the passing of her husband.

The three men set to work digging with a will while Hawk, with that quiet efficiency for which he was famous, wrapped his wife in her best linen sheets, giving her one final kiss and embrace before sewing her into the cloth.

He carried her down to the newly dug grave with the help of Clay, who was a big, solid man easily capable of carrying double that weight on his own. He was aware of a spreading numbness in his body that seemed to start at the top of his head and go down to his feet. He felt as if it were someone else who put his wife into her last resting place along with the rest of the men. He picked up one of the shovels, but Clay gently took him by the shoulders and sat him on the wall, then the three cowboys took up their shovels and buried the woman they had known since they were boys.

Once they were finished, as if he had been rehearsing for days, Hawk came forward and said the words from scripture that they all knew, beginning with the words 'ashes to ashes'. It was not the first time that they had been close to death in the course of their work, and every one of them had a copy of the Bible in their quarters. They had all – even Hawk who had had much of the knowledge of his ancestors passed down to him – been taught scripture in their early years.

The men stood there with their heads bowed while Hawk said his final prayers to his wife. He ended with a short chant from his Blackfoot ancestors. As he did so the sky darkened and the rain began to fall steadily on his barely protected shoulders. He suddenly seemed thinner than before and much older than his years.

'Where's Rye?' asked Holt. 'He oughter know.' Hawk turned and walked from the family graveyard with his men. His lips twisted as he looked at his employee and friend.

'We need to talk,' he said.

CHAPTER THREE

Consciousness was not the result of a sudden wakening. He was dimly aware that he was slung across the back of a horse like a sack of potatoes. The knot inside his stomach that was there from the effects of the chloroform was nothing compared to the way his head felt. Fuzzy was a good description of the sensation in his brain. Each time he gathered his thoughts there would be a bump on the uneven ground that transmitted through the body of his equine transport and jolted away the gathering ideas. His mouth was dry and he could feel a lust arising in him for a drink of water. His hair was long, as black as his father's, and was hanging down in front of his face. Gradually he realized that his legs and arms were tied, the knots chafing against his wrists as he bumped over the ground. At this rate the skin would be red raw.

'Hey, looks like he's waking,' said a familiar voice. The horses were halted. Ryan, the man trussed up like tomorrow's turkey dinner, was even more dimly aware that he was in woodlands, and that rain was hitting the

19

leaves of the oaks and pines, some splashing down on his already soaking back. There was a crunch of snapping branches as a heavy man walked across from his own steed, grabbed Ryan by the hair of his head and looked directly into his face. 'You with us, then?' The speaker had sickly sweet breath laced with coffee and some variety of rotgut whisky. With a shock Ryan recognized Yancey Barnes, the simpleton who many employed and even more scorned.

'You with us, boy? Well, that's good news for us; be much quicker now. I am going to untie you. Don't you try nothing stupid.'

Ryan said nothing. He did not even have enough reactive force in him to hate the man. 'Let me go,' he croaked, 'this is mad.'

'That is as it might be,' said Yancey, hooking Ryan off the saddle efficiently and flinging him to the thorny ground, straddling him like a bear and untying the ropes. He thrust out a hand, which seemed to have been modelled on the animal he so resembled, and grabbed Ryan, who was not a small man, by the back of his shirt and lifted him to his feet. He held on as Ryan's legs buckled, preventing him from falling back down.

He was facing three individuals now, all of whom had dismounted from their own steeds and were staring at him as if he were an exhibit in a freak show. Expecting bandits, his eyes widened in shock as he looked on them, two men and a woman. One of the men, with a cheek full of chewing tobacco, expectorated a brown stream of liquid at Ryan's feet, the other two grinning as the young man pulled back against Yancey's grip.

'Welcome to your nightmare, cousin,' said his kidnapper.

'I need to find him,' said Hawk. 'I'll set out in less than an hour.' He looked at his men almost defiantly. They had the grace to look back at him and reflect the truth through Frank Flynn.

'Boss, you ain't going nowhere. Look at the state of you; your eyes have bags under them you could pack a wadrobe fulla clothes in, and you're exhausted. You're in a perfect state to be killed by whatever bastards have taken your boy.'

'I'll get him back,' said Hawk briefly.

'Look, get some sleep, as much as you can. Rest for a few hours and we'll go into the village and get a posse together. We'll do that right away, and we'll look for them miscreants that took your boy.'

'I'll take no rest. There won't be any rest for me while my boy's out there.' Without another word, Hawk returned to the ranch and began to pack the essentials he would need for the trip. Clay, Flynn and Holt had remained down by the bunkhouse for the moment but he was aware that they were discussing the matter deeply with each other. Hawk was essentially a man of peace, but he brought with him his two Colt pistols along with plenty of bullets, and a Winchester '73, one of the most popular rifles that had ever been produced in the States: an essential for any expedition. He had killed wolves, bears and cougars in his time, but now it was time to hunt the worst enemy of all: man. As he emerged at the stables wearing his long woollen coat, he tucked the pistols into

21

either side. His deep pockets were the right place for them to go: he didn't have a gun belt and holsters like some fancy sheriff, and pockets were good enough for him.

He led out his deep chestnut gelding, whose name was Swift, denoting the fact that he could eat up the miles with his sturdy legs without seeming to lose any stamina. Hawk saddled up with an ease borne of long practice and slid his Winchester into a sheath on his saddle, a statement of intent.

His three men saddled up too, their horses already waiting for them down by the bunkhouse.

'We'll do what you say,' said Hawk. 'We'll go into the village and see if we can get some more help. The wider the spread the more chance of catching the ones who did this.' He said nothing else but trotted off on his horse so quickly that the rest had difficulty keeping up with him. Hawk had not mentioned to them that he had a little secret concealed in one of his saddle bags: over two thousand dollars in paper and coin that he used for running the ranch and for his savings. He had more money in the bank but this would do to start with. Money meant very little to him right now; it was just a tool to be used, and the use for it was to get his boy back.

The ranch was situated just over two miles from the village, not a great distance considering the size of the area. As they came over the hill, beside the river, it became clear at once that there was something wrong. Normally Main Street would have been bustling with people: the village was used for supplies for all the ranches, the hardware store and the livery were always busy, and the saloon was as well, popular as it was with the cowboys who worked in the outlying ranches who were never shy of slaking their thirst within its walls.

Not that the saloon had any walls to speak of: it was a burned-out shell and it stood there as a stark reminder of how quickly destruction could come to a town. Knots of travellers stood here and there in surprised conversation, and the arrival of the new riders spurred the drawing of various weapons, put away when it was seen that they had a different intent.

'What the hell happened here, Joe?' asked Hawk, speaking to one of his fellow ranchers, a big, normally taciturn man called Lamington, who seemed as stunned as the rest.

'We don't rightly know, Hawk,' said Lamington. For some reason he and his fellow ranchers normally called Hawk by his second name, but it was more a reflection of the quality of the word rather than some deliberate insult. 'But they're mostly gone.'

'Gone?'

'The villagers, all of 'em, 'cept for a few bedridden and young 'uns, all gone.'

Holt and Flynn looked at their leader: they were thinking the same thing. Clay wasn't there; he was poking about the ruins of the saloon, being a natural raker. He was being given the news by men who were carrying out a similar act.

'Look at this,' said Clay, returning with a faint air of triumph. He slid up his sleeve to show it was concealing an intact bottle of Scotch whisky. 'Somethin' from the wreckage,' he said.

'Where were they taken?' asked Hawk with a trace of harshness in his voice.

'That is the question.' Lamington scratched his head. 'Guess they was led away real fast by whoever did this. Could've been Indians,' he squinted a little at Hawk as he said this.

'No,' said Hawk, 'if it were the Cherokee they would have simply killed where they were. They don't take prisoners.' No one questioned this opinion.

'What are you going to do now?' asked Clay. 'It's pretty hopeless, ain't it?'

Hawk did not answer him, but walked down the street and looked at the ground with some care. It did not escape him that the body of the trading post keeper, Linton Stack, was lying in between two of the buildings with multiple bullet wounds in his once sturdy frame. He came back to his men. 'It's easy enough to see. They went up into the hills through the woodlands at the edge of town; that in itself is not hard to see.'

'How many?' asked Holt, with an expression of eagerness; he really wanted to know.

'A great many of them,' said Hawk in a voice that did not seem to take in the magnitude of what he was saying. 'Thirty or forty at least, maybe more.' His expression was haunted as he looked at Clay, Holt and Flynn. 'The numbers don't matter, and I'm going after what is mine.'

CHAPTER FOUR

Ryan did not recognize the young woman. She had hair that seemed to be fair, but it was hard to tell because she did not look as if she had washed in a long time. The two men with her were not much older than Ryan, and he knew them both. One was Scott McArthur, his older cousin, and the other was Mack Jardine, a friend of his cousin whom he had known when they had played together as children. They were moving along together through the green woodlands, and he could hear the roaring of the river nearby, which made him wonder why they were heading for the water. The horses were being led by the two men, but the young woman was walking, and so was Yancey. Ryan, despite the fuzziness in his head, was able to keep up with them, powered by the strength of his young body.

The reason why they were heading for the river was soon made clear. The Brazos was not one of those waters usually clear of obstructions, and the village had not been called Hatton Falls for nothing. Upstream, away from the weir that had given the village its name, the river widened out and rushed around an island right in the middle of the water.

At the banks of the river was a rowing boat with two sets of wooden oars, a craft that was big enough for all five of them. McArthur pointed a pistol at Ryan. The weapon looked as if it was a large calibre revolver, old but deadly enough for his purpose.

'You and the big man, you're rowing,' he said, 'now push it out.' Ryan started to obey, noticing that the rowing boat was anchored to the bank by a rope attached to a post. This was an opportunity for him to escape; one of his abilities was being able to swim like a seal, darting through the water. But his head was throbbing and he still felt faintly dizzy, which meant that there was a distinct possibility that he might be swept away by the power of the weir, which was not that far away, and swept to his death on the rocks below. The other young men climbed aboard, and for a moment it looked as if the girl was going to refuse, but Scott gave her a severe look and she bowed her head and climbed aboard. Once Yancey had followed – and he too had a touch of uneasiness in his manner – Ryan took up a pair of the oars and sat at the stern of the boat while Yancey took the other set of oars, released the rope and began to row with a vigour that showed the strength of his mighty body.

Ryan knew that he had to pull too; the weight of the passengers and the force of the river mean that they would soon be pulled into the current if they did not fight the force of the swirling waters around them. He could feel the spray hit his lips as they rowed, but their efforts finally bore some fruit and they were at the island.

From the shore their destination had looked like a vague green and brown shape in the middle of the river, but now they could see that it was much larger than it had seemed on first sight. The river was not just long; it was wide, so that they were already more than 500 feet from the banks and woodlands. The boat pulled up on the shore of the island. Scott jumped out with an eagerness that was perhaps prompted by his lack of enthusiasm for the river than the need for overseeing his prisoner. He jerked his gun at Ryan.

'You,' he said, 'get this pulled up. Help him, Yancey.' Together the two men pulled the boat inwards on the sandbar that made up this side of the island so that it was in no danger of drifting off. The girl was between the two men. She was slim and silent and had drifted out of the boat like a ghost.

'Go forward,' ordered Scott. 'Gee, if it wasn't so much trouble you'd be a dead man by now, Rye boy.'

They were all on the island now. It was surprisingly large, much larger than it had seemed from the shore and sparked a flash of recognition in Ryan.

'This is Shrine Island,' he said. 'It's where the Cherokee come to worship their gods. This ain't a safe place for any of us.'

'For you, you mean, cousin,' said Scott. 'Come on, move.' He brandished his pistol as he said this and there was a gleam in his eyes that said he was not about to listen to any kind of reason.

To his surprise, Ryan discovered that there was a lean-to in the middle of the island, a type of shack that had been constructed hastily from clapboard and roofed with

27

local materials. These were easily found; the silt and dirt that washed down the river was rich in minerals, and the island was covered in lush vegetation with large trees that went almost down to the shore. The interior was rich, green and steamy. Scott gestured to them again and they went inside the interior of the building. It was dank inside with little in the way of furnishings.

'This is where you'll wait,' he said. 'You can yell for help all you want, ain't no one going to hear you. Turn around.'

Ryan, who had been thinking about escape, did as he was told, and turned around only to have his wrists bound together. He was pushed down into a corner and, still dizzy from the chloroform, he fell heavily to the ground. He twisted around where he lay and glared up at his captives.

'You won't get away with this, Scott, or you, Mack. Yancey, they're just using you.'

'Can it,' snapped Scott and booted his cousin in the ribs, making Ryan groan in pain. 'Been wanting to do that for a long time, cousin. Come on, boys.' He started to march out, with the girl following in a lacklustre way.

'Taking her too?' asked Mack.

' 'Course not,' snapped Scott. He grabbed hold of the girl and stared into her face. 'You stay here. Don't set him free or you'll get more of the same.' Mack snickered at this.

'Maybe he'll give her more of the same.'

'Don't matter, she can't come with us.' He pushed the girl and she fell away from him and backed against one of the mouldy walls. She sank slowly to the ground, on the opposite side of Ryan, and stared blankly ahead. McArthur gave one final, derisive laugh and left with his two companions. Straining his ears, Ryan thought he heard a faint noise as the boat was launched, then he heard the splashing of oars in the water. Their captors were gone.

'What's your name?' he asked the girl. She did not respond and he looked at her from his low position. 'Can you help me get free?' Still nothing: for all she was responding he might as well have been invisible. 'What's your name?' he asked again, and this time she pulled away from him as much as she could, into the furthest corner and sat there with her legs drawn tightly together, rocking back and forth.

Hawk was not the kind of man who could lay bare his thoughts. Like many of the Sioux from whom he was descended he saw his way of being that of a man, and men did not think too much about what they were doing and why: they simply took action.

'I'm going back to the ranch,' he said. 'You can come with me.' His men looked at him in a way that he had never seen before, an expression of disbelief.

'But you have to get on the trail after these here miscreants,' said Flynn, not a man to mince his words. 'They've got your boy, after all.'

'He's right,' said Holt. 'It's obvious that they're a powerful bunch, but we can't let them get away with this; we'll get a posse together, made up of the local riders and get after them.'

'I'm in, too,' added Clay. 'There was a girl down in the

village, Lena, she was kinda sweet on me . . . That's her paw lying over there. I guess I know what I have to do.'

'The three of you should come with me,' said Hawk. 'I am looking in the true way for my son.' He looked expectantly at their faces and saw some signs of rebellion. 'Very well, if that is the way then I'll do this on my own. It's a pity after all we meant together. You were good workers and you will hunt down these bandits well.' He was soon on his gelding and riding away from them with no further explanation, not the kind of man to beg or demand.

It wasn't long before he was over the wide slope of land and through the trees before the plains opened in front of him. He was filled with a sorrow that he could not put into words, as if a stone had been placed in the middle of his body and was weighing him down. He could not put into words the depths of his feelings.

He was alone now. Being alone did not trouble him that much – it was the condition that he had known since birth – but he was already missing the companionship of the woman who had walked with him through his adult life. She would have known what to do about their son, and she would have discussed the idea he had in his head about what had been done to him. There was a grim, fixed look about him. He had never been the kind of man who smiled easily, and now there was an expression on his face that promised a hard fight for those who had taken his son. He had not told his ideas to the men in the village because the enormity of what had happened there had made his own concerns fade into the background, but it was his own problems that he had to solve,

30

with or without the help of anyone else. Besides, he had ideas that those in Hatton Falls might have ... not mocked, because no one would mock a grieving man, but would certainly consider fanciful given what had happened.

Then he heard the sound of horses behind him. This was bandit country and he was on a rising slope of land that slowed down his steed. He halted Swift and dived behind a line of rocks on the plain that were big grey things, taller than a man. He reached into his pockets and pulled out his guns, ready to take on whomever was riding after him. Three riders appeared, but they were his own men. They drew up their steeds as he stepped out from behind the rocks.

'What the hell?' he asked.

Clay was the first one to speak. 'When you rode off like that we started to get worried about what you might do. We was all set to ride after the bandits and them villagers, but we kind of got to talking amongst ourselves and thought we'd best stick with you and whatever fool notions you might of got in your head.'

He got on his horse and they rode back towards the ranch. When they arrived, the owner looked around grimly. No one had been there yet, but in his mind it was only a matter of time.

'I'm going to tell the three of you plainly what I think has happened here,' said Hawk. 'My son's been kidnapped. Whoever did this was out for personal gain.'

'But what about the bandits, boss?' asked Holt.

'They took a whole village,' said Flynn, 'so they could take your son too.'

31

'See, that's the thing,' said Hawk, 'if it was just for their purposes they would've taken Rye, but I tell you plainly, they would have killed me there and then. The only thing that makes sense is that my boy was kidnapped.'

'But why?' asked Clay.

'For the most basic reason of all: money,' answered his employer.

CHAPTER FIVE

Aguste Rivero was not a man who compromised his vision. He had his men supervise the newly recruited villagers through the passes and trails that led beside the river for a whole day, until he thought they were well away from any potential pursuers. The fact that the village was so remote, a settlement near the Brazos and living off one of its tributaries, was a factor in his favour. It would be late in the morning before any kind of alarm was raised. These people did not have modern communications like the telegraph: this country was too remote for that kind of innovation, and so no one would have been alerted and warned.

His chief officer, Juan Ramirez, had expressed a strong opinion about what they should have done in the village.

'We should have killed the gringos, shot or stabbed every single one of them, leaving the bodies – a plain show of what we are.'

'I agree with you,' said Rivero, 'that would indeed have been a show of strength, but a pointless one.'

'Instead we are now tasked with overseeing these people who are little more than children in their moaning, sobbing and crying and dragging their heels.' Ramirez held up a short whip. 'Luckily my men have these. They have been helpful in spurring them on.'

'It is what they deserve,' said Rivero, 'and a lot more will suffer a great deal on both sides before we win our republic.'

Most of the villagers obeyed. When one or the other tried to resist they were given a taste of the whip and that brought them back into line. The formation of the column was a great help in keeping the prisoners subdued. At the back rode about twelve of their captors, meaning that anyone breaking away and running in that direction would soon be trampled on by hoofs. Another fifteen or so of the men rode alongside the prisoners, making sure they kept up a good pace and making sure that the whips came into play when their captives showed signs of flagging. It soon became clear that they were going to halt for the night when the leader brought them down to an inlet beside the mighty Brazos. This was a place where the water had come in to the shore many times over the years and had created a rocky overhang that allowed for some shelter from the elements. It was only springtime and they had already experienced some light rain. There was plenty of room for them all because the inlet was wide and the overhang was huge.

'Take the fittest of the gringos and make sure that they gather plenty of firewood,' said Rivero. 'You will have to untie their hands to do this, but if they run off, shoot them in the back and do it quickly; we can't allow any to

34

escape.' His men led off ten of the captured men. Luckily the woodlands around had plenty of fallen branches, the legacy of the storm winds of winter. The men, supervised by their captors, soon made a pile of branches that grew taller than two men down by the shore.

Normally Texas was a state that consisted of huge plains with patches of woodland here and there, but around the river Brazos the woodlands were extensive and deep, with white oaks, beech and pecan trees, pines and many varieties of flowing bushes fighting for space, making the area rich in contrast. There was a reason for this: the river was rich in silt, and every year when the rains were heavy the river Brazos became a monster that burst its banks and spread through the surrounding countryside, enriching the soil and creating the conditions for the woodlands to spread.

In the meantime the other soldiers had been using their weapons for hunting game – mostly rabbits, turkeys, ducks and quail, and one or two deer. The troops expertly skinned and prepared these, used the branches and twigs and built several fires along the shoreline, cooking the meat on makeshift spits. The troops ate first and the remnants were flung to the prisoners, who fell upon the scraps of meat as if they were at a banquet.

Once or twice some of the men tried to speak up, but they were silenced immediately by blows from a whip or the butt of a gun.

The prisoners settled down for the night, most of them huddled together for warmth, while the bandits used their ponchos and horse blankets for that purpose. The worst part of the chill was at three in the morning, and some of the prisoners moaned and tried to get more comfort from their fellows. At just about five in the morning the guards were roused, all of them, including some who had nearly fallen asleep during their watch. None of them were in a good mood, either prisoners or their captors, and a few whips were cracked and pain was administered to get them shifted.

The only problem was that some of the prisoners didn't get up, and would indeed never rise again, for they had died from the cold. Rivero looked at the bodies: he had slept in a tent that had been especially erected for him, and was fresh and immaculately dressed.

'Throw the bodies into the woods,' he said. This was done and the half-dozen corpses, including a young boy, were disposed of in a summary manner. The rest were led off, with one woman wailing at the loss of her child. When she was hit with a whip she would not cease wailing, her cries a kind of plaintive tune to the mournful travellers as they shuffled onwards.

Ryan was young and he was fit, fitter than the men who had captured him. He was also a great deal more intelligent than they were, all of which would mean nothing if he was not able to get free before their return. It was obvious that the girl was not going to be much help so he ignored her for the moment and attempted to get up. This was not particularly easy given that his hands were tied behind his back and they had thrown him to the ground. He managed to turn round and pushed his body along, was able to sit up and, by pushing against the ground with his feet, managed to get upright using one of the clapboard walls.

The effects of the chloroform had mostly worn off, although he still had a trace of the nausea it had caused and swayed as he stood up, in distinct danger of falling down again. In the corner opposite him, the girl did not appear to be paying any attention to what he was doing, but she pulled away from him when he walked past her. He raised one of his feet and kicked the door. It was not well secured and at the blow the whole building shook as if it was going to fall down around their ears. The girl scuttled away from him on her hands and knees, but he was still ignoring her, concentrating on what had to be done.

He was out in the open. The shack had been built in the midst of the thick woodland brush that covered the island, but there was a clearing around where they were. One of the trees was an old beech with a knot on the trunk, a rough outgrowth that immediately captured his attention. He went over to this, turned around and sawed away at the ropes. It was a hot day and the sweat was pouring down his face. He thought at first that nothing was happening and for a short while a flood of despair filled his body. What was the point of doing anything? He was trapped on an island with a woman who seemed an imbecile and there was no way of getting to the mainland.

At last, though, he felt some of the fibres parting and the bonds that held him began to loosen. It was remarkable to him that having his arms free was so liberating, but now when his enemies came back he could hide and ambush them.

He was going to go off and explore the island when he remembered the girl. She was easy to forget because it was obvious that she did not want to speak to anyone or even make her presence felt. She might be useful if they were going to try and get away from their captivity. He went inside the shack and saw that she was facing the door with her back to the wall. As he entered, wholly free now, she scrambled to her feet. It was obvious that at the first opportunity she would try to scramble past him like a startled deer.

'Look,' he held up his hands to show that he was weapon free, 'I don't know who you are or what they've done to you, but we're here together. I want to help you, and maybe you can help me.' He noticed that she was looking at his face as he spoke, her eyes wide, but still ready to run. 'Have they hurt you? What have they done to you? I want to help, I really do.' Then he stopped talking as he looked into her frightened face. Then he was aware of how helpless he felt. He had been brought up to be a man, and although he had been friendly with a girl in the village, the only woman he had known well was his mother. Like his father, she had told him that a true man never offered violence towards a woman. He was eighteen years old and in some ways he was as help-less as she was. His eyes fell from her face and he looked at the ground.

'I guess that I can't do much for you. If you want to see what we can do, then come with me and we'll beat 'em.' There was no answer, so he turned and left her alone and walked out of the door. He did not know when his kid-nappers were going to return but he would have to look around and make his plans before they did return. Then he heard a footfall behind him and a soft voice.

'Wait,' said the girl.

CHAPTER SIX

When the riders came to the ranch they found out that a note had been pinned to the main door. Hawk spotted it at once. It was scrawled on the back of an old grocery bill and the message was brief and chilling. The other men crowded around Hawk and looked at the words with gathering anger:

We hav yore boy. Bring a ransom of fifteen hundred to three forks trail at six the day or else he gets it dont try any tricks or his throt is cut.

Hawk looked at the piece paper with a cold fury on his face as if it was the men who had abducted his son. It was an expression that showed he was not about to give them what they wanted without some kind of fight.

'This is someone who knows me and knows the area,' he said. 'This isn't just some kind of chance kidnap by a bunch of Mexicans.'

'Mighty risky of them to come right up to your door,' said Holt.

'Not really, they would have guessed that we would be out looking for them. It was when we were down in the village; it struck me that whoever had committed the mass abduction would not have come to one specific ranch to kidnap one person. They – the bandits I mean – were making a statement with what they have done, one that's political. If they had kidnapped one person it would have been the son of a local politician or a judge.'

His men looked at him with new respect. In the past their employer had been nicknamed Hawk of the Hills, a semi-mocking name from his habit of going the extra mile or three for his business, and now they could see how the name had come about.

'Well, what are you going to do?' asked Holt.

'We're not going to wait around for the meeting with these assholes,' said Hawk, 'we're going to look for them right now. They ain't all brain, that's evident from the way they've behaved, and they've asked for a realistic sum of money knowing that's just about what I could lay my hands on right away.'

In a business where the average rider was paid thirty dollars a month, fifteen hundred was a lot of money.

Hawks said nothing else but led his horse to the stables where he took off the saddle and gave it a quick rub down and some oats and molasses, advising his men to do the same. Looking after your horse was probably the best investment a man could make in these parts and they hastily followed suit. On the way out of the stable he looked around the area, his sharp eyes scanning for signs of who had been there.

'They've got horses,' he said. 'I can see some distinct

41

hoof marks, and badly shod they are. We'll get some coffee and fry up a bit of grub, fuel for the time ahead. As for the cattle, well we'll just have to let 'em go for the moment. This is more urgent, so urgent we have to take our time over it.'

It was then that they understood the wisdom of the old expression 'more haste, less speed'. By feeding the horses and his men he was fuelling a search that would lead quickly to the results that he wanted, but he did not lead them into his home, preferring to stay with his men and eat at the bunkhouse. Going into his home right now was too painful, too full of memories, and he had to remain strong right now and do what had to be done.

After some cornbread and coffee, Hawk sat with his men. His head drooped and he slept for the first time since he had woken from the blow to his head. The others marvelled at the fact that he could do this at all, but it was a talent he had from his early days. He awoke, stood up and stretched his lithe body.

'Guess it's time we hit the trail and deal with whoever has my boy.' The words were few, but looking at the cold expression on his face when he said the words, none of the men present would have changed places with the kidnappers.

In the meantime, Ryan was with the girl on Shrine Island. She was still standing at a distance from him, and they were still wasting time talking, except as far as he was concerned it was time well spend considering the fact that she might very well be able to help him escape from their predicament.

'My name is Abbey Jones,' said the girl. 'I grew up in Houston, which is growing all the time. My father was a senator and always away from home. Then when I was nine he died in a coach accident. A couple of years later my mother died as well, of scarlet fever. There was an epidemic at the time. I grew ill, too, and I nearly died, but I recovered and I was sent to live with a rich aunt and uncle in the west of the city.' She had a soft voice, so that often Ryan had to strain to hear what was being said, but he gave her the courtesy of listening intently to her words.

'When I was growing up I thought the world was a wonderful place. Even when my father died, life was fine, even though I missed him. The trouble was, being a politician, he was always away from home anyway, so I could pretend for a while that he was somewhere else and wasn't really dead. But when my mother passed on, I was in despair.'

'Did your aunt and uncle look after you well?' He regretted asking the question as soon as it left his lips. Her face was white beneath the grime.

'How are you going to get us off this island?' she asked in a faltering voice.

He was quite a forthright person, a trait he had inherited from his father, but he could sense there was no point pressing her on the matter. 'I guess what we should do is take in the lie of the land,' he said. 'Let's explore and see what's in this place.'

She had kept her distance from him even though they were conversing with each other now. As he moved off she still kept from coming too close to him. No wonder the men who had brought her here had left her untied, he thought, it was obvious that she would never have tried to escape on her own. Yet for all he knew her behaviour was some kind of act and she had a gun beneath that somewhat plain dress she was wearing.

It was obvious, even after a short search, that there was nothing on the island that resembled a boat, except for the rotting frame of an old canoe. In the same area he found a rusty old knife, however, and an axe. What they also found, though, was a totem pole of the kind venerated by the Indians. It had some wonderful carvings on it of faces with native characteristics, bears and even a bald eagle atop. This was probably the reason why this area was called Shrine Island, and was a cause for concern. Not all of the tribes in this area had been placed in reservations and Ryan had the sudden thought that if they were around they might take a dim view of intruders in their holy space. It was a thought that sent a shiver running through him because he was well aware of what the Indians were capable of in defending what they saw as theirs. The girl looked at the religious artefact without much concern, not knowing what it signified.

'There's no way of getting off, is there?' she asked, still keeping her distance from him.

'Well, at least there's plenty of water,' he said. 'We won't die of thirst. I detected rabbits and ducks and turkeys, there's fish in the river, and I noticed there was some basic hunting gear in the lean-to. I can make fire by getting dry grass and striking flint against a bit of old iron or steel, getting a flame and building a fire down at the shoreline. We won't starve either.'

44

'You can get fire and feed us?' she asked looking at him as if he had two heads.

'Sure,' said Ryan with a confidence he did not feel. 'It was the way I was brought up. There's always a way of fighting back.' He looked at the waters rushing past the island and fell silent. The wooded shoreline was temptingly close and he was a powerful swimmer. His biggest worry was that the waters would carry him down to the very falls that gave the village its name. However, on this side of the island, they were not only closer to the shore: there was a bend in the river that the waters swept around, with the far shore jutting out like an isthmus from the mainland. If he had some sort of craft and they could steer in the right direction there was a possibility they could catch the shore. He stood there so long with the wheels of his mind turning that the girl gave an impatient shout and his head cleared.

'Can we get out of here?' she asked. 'You said yourself there might be Indians. Can you light that fire you were talking about and get us some food?' He looked at her, deciding that perhaps this was not the time to let her know what was on his mind.

'We'll try,' he said.

CHAPTER SEVEN

The villagers found themselves being led towards a place that looked as if it should not have been there. It was a long grey wall built from a mixture of adobe and brick, a wall that was obviously part of a bigger structure, but which they were approaching from a low level so that they could see little more than that side. It was situated close to the mighty Brazos so that the waters could still be heard rushing past, but was a few hundred feet from the river itself, tucked amongst the Pinto hills. A place this vast could only have been built by the government, and the age of the place told its own story. They were toiling upwards to the structure from the lowlands at the river's edge. One of the villagers, a man in his fifties looked at the building and gave a faint groan. The people walking with him looked at him covertly to avoid the attentions of the men with whips.

'What is it, Bert?' asked a stick-thin woman called Aimee who had run the village inn, a place where weary travellers could buy a bite to eat and grab a place to sleep. Her business had been quiet to begin with, but thrived during the cattle drives and it was rumoured that as a widow she hadn't been too fussy about shaking off the attentions of the cowboys.

'Camp Brazos,' said Bert, a stocky man who looked as if he would have keeled over in the first ten miles but who had somehow survived well. 'Used as a prisoner of war camp during the Civil War.'

'Shut it up, gringo,' said their overseer, who was riding beside them, a swarthy Mexican with a fierce moustache, who waved his quirt at them and caught Bert on the shoulder with a lash of the leather. The villager winced in pain and went quiet, the expression on his broad features showing that he was storing up a degree of resentment for later.

The walls of the camp were closer now and it was obvious that the place had seen much better times. The gates of the former internment camp were opened and the villagers were prodded and pushed into line by their guards and made to go inside. None of the captured villagers were sure of what they were going to see, even the man who had known that they were entering a type of prison did not know what was inside, merely that the camp existed. From the start the impression was that of a big parade area of the kind beloved by all military institutions. In the centre of this square was a flagpole, which was a sorry looking sight given that it was totally bereft of a single banner.

At the head of the rectangular military parade ground was a fort that was raised several storeys high. It was a plain building that had once had whitewashed walls but was now an uneven grey with peeling paint evidence of past glories. To one side of this was a barracks that would have housed the soldiers who had guarded both the installation and their prisoners. To the other was the stabling for the horses, and those guards who had entered first dismounted and stood beside their horses, their guns at the ready as the prisoners were driven forward.

As for the prisoners themselves, their accommodation was to be a great deal more basic. To either side of the parade ground was what could only be described as a holding area. During the Civil War, commanders had been under pressure to make a place where their prisoners could be kept and Camp Brazos, although large, was constructed in an extremely basic manner. There had been no time to construct cells and make a prison near the river. These camps were supposed to be places where people would be held for short periods of time while they were awaiting trial, and reassigned to a proper prison away from the scene of military conflict. They were also places from which people could be plucked and shot if that was considered necessary.

The compounds were simply areas that had been fenced off from the rest of the camp. They were mostly open and had little in the way of seating except for stone blocks set at regular intervals. At the back of the compound, which was at least fifty feet wide and a couple of hundred feet long, was what passed for accommodation, areas where walls had been built much lower than the height of the prison camp and roofed over with wooden boards. There were only six of these to each compound and they were open to the front so that every movement

48

of the prisoners could be seen.

There was no sign of traditional bedding, although some loose bales of straw had been thrown inside to be divided by the prisoners, to give them something to lie on. Near the front were water troughs like those used by horses, but it was plain that these could be filled from outside the fence, although they were already full. One of the compounds was sealed from the rest of the camp by a long metal fence with the newly invented barbed wire at the top.

The other compound was bare and some of the rusty fencing had been used to restore parts of the other side, where the prisoners were to be kept. The walls at the back of the damaged area were crumbling.

The fenced-in area had a metal gate that was the only new-looking part of the construction besides the barbed wire. This was opened and the prisoners were herded inside, with one or two making a feeble effort to resist. One man was clubbed to the ground and booted in the ribs by a large Mexican who looked as if he might have continued to kick until the man was dead, but was restrained by a stern look and a cry of 'detener,' from Rivero, who despite his position was supervising the whole process closely. The injured man was flung inside with the rest.

When his prisoners were sealed in, they were ignored for the moment while many of the other horses and men entered and the animals were stabled. Not all of the men and horses had been brought inside, and it was obvious that men would be needed to patrol the area and to create hunting parties that would go out and forage for food. Only when he had seen that the fort was set up to his satisfaction did Rivero reappear with Ramirez, flanked by guards with guns who dwarfed them. The prisoners, most of them, were lying down. Some of the more enterprising had created makeshift beds in the bedding areas from the straw that had been left.

'Come forward, you filthy American dogs,' said Rivero, who was not a man to mince his words or conceal his attitudes. When the prisoners did not come forward fast enough he nodded to one of the men beside him and that individual fired a few bullets that kicked up dust near the recumbent figures that had not yet risen and made them come forward hastily.

'You American dogs wonder why we have done this,' said their captor. He gave a grin that was totally devoid of humour. 'You have taken large areas of my homeland and that of my people, you settle here on land that was ours for generations. These hills belonged to my ancestors. They are rich in gold, copper, zinc and other metals, yet all this is no longer considered mine, but belongs to your filthy government.'

'He tells the truth,' said Ramirez, with a serious nod. 'You are invaders, not us.'

'That is why you are here. I have used money from my family to come here, with the men who believe in my cause,' said Rivero, 'and together we will take back what is mine.'

'But why us?' asked Bert, shaking the bars. 'We can't do anything for you.'

'You can't, señor?' asked Rivero. He looked around at the crumbling walls. 'You can build, can't you? All of you can.'

50

*

Hawk was not one to unburden his feelings. His face was expressionless as he rode around the area of the ranch looking for clues as to what had happened. He examined the soil with some thought and then came to some conclusions that he shared with his men.

'There's three of them, and I know for a fact that one of them was Yancey.' He looked out towards the huge sloping fields that led down from his ranch. These were busy with cattle, big black and white longhorns that were feeding well on the crisp spring grass. These were not the focus of his attention; instead he was looking at the woodlands beyond the fields, knowing that beyond this was the river that dominated the area. He was using line of sight and that seemed good enough to him.

'I reckon they didn't mess around,' he said. 'Yancey and one of them came up here in the early hours. Yancey knew that I liked to sit on the porch, so they would have been in place before I arrived. Any movements would have been concealed by the soft, new grass and the sound of them restless cattle.'

'Why didn't they just rob you?' asked Holt.

'Because they wouldn't have known where the money was,' said Hawk, thinking of the spot in his home, under the floor in the front room in the left corner beneath a cabinet. Almost certainly it would have been a hard place for them to find his money, especially at that time of the morning. Besides, there was something else going on here. 'I feel as if they were homing in on me like some kind of target, as if I had a big blue circle on me,' he

51

added. 'I can't explain why, but that's what it's like.'

'But what reason would they have?' asked Clay.

'Regardless, I'm on their track, and with your help I'm going to get them,' said Hawk.

'Surely the best way to deal with this would be to take the ransom to Three Forks and wait,' said Clay. 'Then you could attack them then and force them to tell you where your boy is.'

'Not the best way,' Hawk shook his head and gazed upon his three men. They were all standing beside their mounts at the headland of the ranch, gazing down at the thick woodlands across the green expanse before them. 'The reason is that they'll use Yancey, and if he doesn't come back they'll get off with their freedom and we'll never find him.'

'This way seems kind of filled with chance,' said Holt.

'Have you ever been in the same room as a wasp?' asked Hawk. 'We all have. Well, see that critter? He's mighty mad at being trapped in there, and he gets madder and madder all the time and his brain ain't that mighty. You might open a door or window and try to get him out, but he's so mad at you that, despite trying to help him, he's going to sting you just to get rid of his madness. Well, what you've got to do is roll up a newspaper and whack him on the head before he gets to that stage. That's what we're doing. We strike now and we do it well.'

On his instructions the four of them fanned out but still followed a direct line of sight from the ranch. The cows looked at them with some kind of respect and curiosity because they were used to being herded, with one or two even coming towards the riders, but a quick 'holah' from the riders and a wave of the quirt was enough to disperse them. Hawk feared that this might alert the kidnappers but it was something that had to be done.

Finally, when they arrived at the tree line, they dismounted from their steeds, took out their guns and walked amidst the foliage.

With his acute senses, Hawk was able to detect the smell of recently burned charcoal long before his companions. Dressed in his long greenish-grey coat with a grey felt hat on his head with a jay's feather stuck in the band, his slow movements and ability to slide through the undergrowth, barely cracking a twig in the process, meant that he was able to find the camp belonging to the intruders before the rest of his men.

They had set up quite a little home from home in a clearing in the forest, but still sheltered by the oaks, pines and beech trees that so happily intermingled in the rich soil close to the river. They had two canvas tents, both of which looked as if they had been bought cheaply from previous owners, probably prospectors, and both of which had been patched several times. In addition, they had wisely built a fire in the middle of the clearing by surrounding it with large stones so that the flames would not escape and set their surroundings on fire. He could even smell the coffee brewing in a tin can sat amid the glowing coals. They were not too bothered about telltale smoke giving away their position, given that it was trapped by the thick green canopy above them.

Hawk had been hoping that this situation would be

resolved right then and there, and as Clay arrived, Hawk signalled to him to come to a halt. Clay was a big man and would seriously alarm the three individuals who were currently seated around the fire. There was no sign of his son. Ryan might have been a prisoner tied up inside one of the tents, except the way these were situated they were face-on to him, with their fronts tied back to keep them aired in the hot day, and he could see they only contained bedrolls and some weapons. If they attacked and killed the three men right now they might never know where his son was, and that would defeat the exercise.

Hawk gave a nod of his head to Clay and the big man understood exactly what to do. The other riders were on the far side of the camp. They too would follow his lead.

Hawk stepped forward, gun in either hand. 'I guess you boys have got a bit of explaining to do.' He hefted one of his guns as Jardine scrambled for his weapons. 'I wouldn't do that, else you want your head to part from your shoulders.' Jardine halted where he was, all the fight out of him, but the other two men turned and faced Hawk. One was the huge figure of Yancey Barnes, but it was the other man who drew his immediate attention.

'Scott? What the hell are you up to?'

'Never mind,' snarled McArthur. 'Yancey, rip his head off.' With a snarl the big man threw his body forward, doing as he was told.

CHAPTER EIGHT

'You're going to do what?' asked the girl again. They were back at the lean-to and had finished a meal of cooked duck, of which there were plenty on the island. The girl had turned pale when Ryan trapped the animal before it could get into the water, but he had broken its neck with a degree of efficiency that showed he had done the same kind of thing before, not just once but many times.

'Paw always says there's no reason why a man should starve when he's surrounded by plenty,' said Ryan at the time. He had used the knife he had found to prepare his catch and she had robbed him of her presence while he was doing so, unable to bear the reality of what he was doing. But the smell of cooking had brought her back to his fire in front of the makeshift building and she had eaten ravenously as if she had not been fed for a while. He had found some edible plant leaves – a form of wild lettuce – and they had eaten the meat wrapped in this like a makeshift taco. It was then that he had made the proposal that had made her stare at him. Not just stare either, but rising and backing away from him as if he was some kind of madman.

'We don't have a boat,' he said reasonably enough, 'but we have plenty of wind-blown and chopped down wood. Some of the trunks are old enough to have dried out without rotting through. They'll float well enough. We can launch ourselves into the river on one and use it as a way of getting to the bank.'

'That's mad,' she said, 'mad; you'll get us both killed.' She was trembling now. She had managed to tidy herself up somehow; she had tied her hair back using some cotton and had cleaned her face in the river. Scrubbed up like that, and sitting across from him, he had thought she was quite pretty. Her features were delicate and refined and she had large, doe-like eyes. He could imagine that her smile would be quite bright, but she had not smiled once since their unfortunate meeting. She was already on her feet, and now she backed away from him even more in the clearing and away from the fire. Her face crumpled and she began to sob, not loud, but quietly, her hand coming to her face as she tried to hide her distress.

Ryan was a young man of tender feelings. He had dispatched a fowl less than an hour before, but he had done it with speed and mercy, and he was not one to make an animal suffer unnecessary pain. Putting down the remnants of his meal, he came forward to try and comfort her in some way, possibly by putting his arms around her – a not unpleasing prospect – but she looked alarmed at his approach and backed away even further, turning briefly to make sure that she had a clear escape route from him.

He had seen the same kind of behaviour in deer when

they were being hunted, but had never thought to see it in another human being.

'Abbey, look here, I ain't going to harm you. I want to look after you, if anything. If you really feel that bad, I'll tell you what, I'll lay in some more meat for you, find some more plants you can eat . . . I saw some wild radishes and green beans; you can eat those raw. Then I'll go on my own and come back for you. I'll just need your help pushing the trunk to the water.' He backed well away from her to prove that he meant her no harm and went back to finish his meal.

She stood there where she was on the far side of the clearing for what seemed like an eternity, the silence between them only broken by the sound of the birds and the clear precise chirruping of the cicadas.

'You think you'll survive?' she asked.

'I know I will,' he said to her with a degree of confidence he did not feel. The truth was, nobody knew what would happen once he was in the water; the current could be so strong it would sweep him right around the bend and down the falls, but he knew that it was better than waiting here at the mercy of his idiot cousin.

'I'll help you then,' she said. There was no time like the present, and although they had just eaten, it would be at least an hour before he would actually enter the water.

The first thing they had to do was locate a suitable piece of wood. He had seen some fallen trees down near the shore. One of these he judged to be large and dried out enough to act as a makeshift canoe, one that had not been hollowed out. The trouble was, it had a few spreading branches. He did not want to risk the knife because he might need it later on, but luckily they had also found an old axe left by some careless former inhabitants – probably the same people who had built the lean-to. The axe might even have been left by Indians, but even so it was so old and rusty, having been half-buried in the sand, that he reckoned its owners had not returned for a long time. He was not about to test the theory.

Instead he went into the island and found a large, solid rock – sandstone was no good for what he wanted to do – and began to rub the blade of the axe back and forth against the grain of the rock, a sharp grating noise ringing through the air as he did so. The girl stood there with her arms folded and watched him.

'Why are you doing this? You already have the axe and the tree you need.'

'Yeah, and I guess I'm trying to make my job a whole lot easier,' he said, continuing with his task. It was only after some ten minutes that he inspected the blade again and gave a grunt of satisfaction. He might have to come back after a while, but the blade was sharp enough to do what he wanted at that moment. It was a hand-axe with a handle made of solid cherry wood. He recognized the grain, and had used such tools before in his work on the ranch.

They went back and the girl began to break off some of the branches near the top of the tree, at which point Ryan stopped her.

'Abbey, I know you're helping and all, but there's no point doing that. You're just making work for yourself.'

'Well leave them on,' she said, 'what's the point of

stripping them off at all?'

'The point is that the spreading branches make the whole thing unstable,' said Ryan, 'I guess it's got something to do with catching the water, but if you've ever seen a tree with all its branches being swept along, the whole thing is being moved, the branches keep catching the flow of water and it whirls around. Look, I'll show you what we need to do.' He went to where one of the branches began at the trunk of the tree. 'See, it's much thicker here, but this is the root of a lot of the spreading branches and twigs that come out. This is what I've got to cut off.'

He did not spend further time on explanations, because he could see that she was hurt at his rejection of her earlier efforts. Normally he would be more sympathetic, but they had a job to do and time was against them.

He did not chop at the node as an amateur might have done. It was about the thickness of a man's leg, and such chopping would have been a long, boring process. Instead he made a v-shaped cut in the wood at one side, followed by another v-cut on the other, then he bore down on the branch from above. Surprisingly, he stopped chopping before the branch was severed from the main trunk.

'Why did you stop before the branch was severed from the main trunk?' she asked.

'Because we have another job to do now and I need a hand from you,' he said. He stood up. His back was aching a little and the muscles in his arms were sore. He put down the axe and showed her where to grab, further

59

along from where he had made the cuts. She grasped the idea instantly, and they acted in unison moving the spreading branches back and forward.

There was a satisfying crack and the branch with all its outspreading offshoots was parted from the main body of the tree. They pulled away their efforts so that they had more room to work. This left them only a couple more to do.

The girl picked up the axe. 'My turn,' she said. Ryan was about to object, but something held him back. She had been watching him intently, and although her arms were slim she was young and strong, and worked with a will. Barely ten minutes later, she too put down the axe and they worked the offshoots back and forth. He grabbed the axe and set to work with renewed vigour, having had a rest while she was chopping, and the last branch was soon dealt with.

This left only a few outgrowths down the trunk and he soon dealt with those. When he stood up he saw that she was still watching him, but this time with interest instead of fear.

'We did it,' she said, 'we got it ready,' and for the first time since they had met she gave a laugh of delight and smiled at him. As he had expected, her smile was pretty too, her laugh a welcome distraction.

'Job well done,' he grinned back at her, 'I could hug you with delight.' He stepped forward, dropping the axe with a soft thud and for a moment he was overwhelmed with a desire to take her in his arms. Moreover, he could see from her slightly parted lips and the look in her eyes that she was not about to resist. Then he tripped slightly over the uneven ground and the moment was gone. She stepped away from him and her wary manner returned.

'Help me roll this down to the water's edge,' he said. She obeyed, looking at him from time to time. It was hard work. He stood up and looked across at the curving mainland.

'Yep,' he said, 'guess this is the right place. I should be carried up against that curve and make landfall.'

'No,' said a choking voice, and his arms were suddenly full of the warm, perspiring girl. 'No, don't.'

CHAPTER NINE

Hawk was not known for his tracking abilities for nothing, and one of those abilities was stealth. As Yancey snarled and ran forward, Hawk stepped backwards and vanished. His attacker stopped in mid-rush and looked bewildered, and that was when Clay took his turn, came forward and put a gun to Yancey's head.

'Stop there, big fella, or you're going to get that crown of yours blown off.' Yancey froze, and the other kidnappers who had started to run in the opposite direction from their would-be captors found that they, too, were under a threat of their own when Flynn and Holt came out of the woods with their own weapons ready.

'Get your hands up, all of you,' said Hawk in a world-weary voice as he stepped forward again. 'Yancey, you made a bad mistake falling in with these two. What the hell's the matter with you? I never figured you as a criminal.'

'Don't say anything.' McArthur looked at Yancey and

shook his head. 'You don't need to say a thing, big stuff.'

'You shut up,' said Hawk. His lips were pulled back thinly across his teeth and it was obvious that there was suppressed fury in his voice. 'Tell me, Yancey.'

'Money,' said the big man. 'Thousands of dollars, that's what they said. A lotta dollars, divided three ways, they said.' He lifted one big hand and tried to count off on his fingers. 'More than them in thousands.'

'Yancey, I'll tell you what they were going to do,' said Hawk. 'They were going to use you to get the kidnap money, then they would've shot you in the head. Your share would've been a bullet to the brain.' This was not some kind of conjecture; this was what he really thought. His black eyes bore into the milky gaze of the bulky man in front of him, and Yancey suddenly seemed to believe what he was being told. The muscles in his broad face began to quiver, and despite the guns on him he turned and looked at McArthur.

'You,' he said, 'you, I'll rip apart, I'll stamp on you.' He gave a roar that resembled the bellow of a particularly angry bull and sprang forward in the direction he was facing.

'He's lying,' said McArthur desperately, 'you're one of us. *Amigos*, the three *amigos*, Yancey.' The big man stopped his advance, looking uncertain again, breathing heavily. Wisely, Hawk's men were keeping out of the argument.

'Ask him what he was going to do with the money, where the two of them were going to go,' said Hawk. 'They were going to go back to the big city. Is that some-where you would belong, Yancey? They were just using you for your strength; they don't care about you at all. No, a bullet to the head is what it would have been.'

There was such calm certainty in Hawk's voice that Yancey believed him and advanced again.

'Don't do anything to them,' said Hawk calmly. 'There's a way of settling this, Yancey; nobody has to get hurt or shot.' Yancey lumbered around again and stared at Hawk with narrowed eyes.

'What be that thing to do, Indian man?' he demanded.

'Just tell me, let me know where my son is, and I'll guarantee that you'll be helped, and even rewarded. Otherwise this could end badly.'

Scott, who had been watching this exchange with a bunched jaw, suddenly lost all caution. He spoke in a voice that seemed to come from a deep, dark well, with a fixed look on his face. 'You . . . You bastard. What you did to my paw, that money, it's mine; all mine. You let him die poor, and you took everything he had.'

'What did he tell you? He had the chance to become a partner in the business. It wasn't my doing that he upped and left for Houston with the family because he couldn't do his work and make it, because of his need for the bottle.'

McArthur, too, gave a roar, and while it was not as deep or as loud as that previously done by Yancey, it was just as heartfelt. He ignored the guns trained on him and ran at the man whom he had targeted. He was not able to go far because Yancey gave a sweep of his big right arm and knocked him to the ground. He gave a groan and tried to get up, but Yancey stood over him with a look that indicated he would not be too pleased if Scott tried to rise.

In the meantime, Jardine looked around at the four grim-looking armed men, the others having stepped into view. The look on his face was one of abject surrender.

'Can I put my arms down?' he asked. 'They're getting tired.'

'Nope, in a minute,' said Hawk, 'but now it's time for business. Where is my son?'

'Don't tell 'em,' groaned Scott from where he lay on the ground, half-sitting and holding his head.

'I don't know who you are, son,' said Hawk, 'but 'less you start to 'fess up this is going to end real badly for you.'

'Don't say a word.'

'Water,' said Yancey suddenly, 'goin' real fast. And the oars made my arms sore.'

'What?'

'You'll never get to him,' said Scott McArthur, a humourless grin spreading across his face. 'He's lost to you.'

Far from being lost, Ryan was stepping away from the not unwelcome touch of a young woman with whom he was trapped.

'I'm sorry,' he said, 'but the truth is, these men are armed. If I had a firearm of some kind I could fend them off, or more sensible like, wait until they landed and challenge 'em for their boat. As it is, all I got is an old knife and an axe, and the knife looks as if it would break with one good blow.'

'That's not what I meant.' Her face was white now, whiter than it had ever been in their short acquaintance. 'I'm going to do it; I'm coming with you.'

He did not say anything or even thank her, but in his heart he was grateful for her desire to come with him. He had not told her so, but he felt that his weight alone would not be enough to prevent the log from sweeping around the bend of the river. However, with the two of them holding on, there was a fighting chance that the weight would be great enough to bear down on their wooden saviour and bring them close enough to the mainland. There was only one way to find out.

'Let's do it then,' he said.

The girl paused and looked at him. 'I just want to know one thing: why does he hate you so much?'

'Who?'

'Scotty, as his pal calls him. Bastard. I saw his face when you were in the boat and when he was tying you up. He really wants to do something bad to you – and he will.'

He saw what she was doing; she was trying to distract them from their immediate peril by speaking of other matters. It was not a ploy he would have welcomed, but the answer surprised him. 'I guess he feels let down and vengeful against my family. He thinks I got everything he should have got and he didn't. I guess he's been on the receiving end of some mighty persuasive rhetoric against me and my kin.'

'From whom?'

'His father, Uncle Wyatt. He was my maw's younger brother. They was close in age really, just a year apart and when he married, she got Granpaw to give him a patch of land and a start on the ranch. There was even talk that through time he would become a partner, but he turned out to be a bent ticket.'

'Why, what happened?'

'Turned out he was a little too fond of the bottle. Liked a bit of a gamble too. The upshot was that just a few years after Scott was born he gambled away the homestead he had been given by Granpaw, who had died in the interim. Me and Scott, we was boys together; played in these hills until we was eight. Mack too, at times.'

'So your father didn't help him?'

'Oh, Paw did what he could, but the ranch went through bad times too. On Maw's persuasion he took off with Scott and my aunt to the big city, and failed there too from what I hear. He went from one job to another and he always failed at those, too, and got involved in some crooked deals. It broke my mother's heart. But he never talked about coming back to ranching. The work is hard and he wasn't going to work hard unless he really needed to.' It was as if he had forgotten where they were, on the shore of an island with the river practically lapping at their feet. 'When Maw heard about Wyatt's death, it set her back. I just hope Paw's hid this business from her; she's real bad just now.'

'No wonder Scott hates you,' she said, 'he sees you as the little golden child who gets everything handed to him on a plate.'

'Then he doesn't know my father,' said Ryan. 'Everything I get, I worked for. I even had to work to pay

67

for my own schooling past fourteen. There's a big world out there; I intend to leave home and get my own business before I'm twenty. Talking about business,' he looked down at their makeshift craft, 'I guess it's time.'

Together they pushed the log into the water at the trajectory he had worked out earlier. They would soon find out whether or not he had made a mistake. The air around them had been fairly warm for the time of year, but the waters that swelled the Brazos came down from the mountains, and the water was so cold that it took their breath away. Luckily, though, they had the presence of mind to continue with their plan and cling to the log.

As he had suspected the whole event was over in one tumultuous rush. The furious waters carried them forward towards the bend in the river, but the log was over twenty feet long and an awkward shape, especially when the two of them were clinging on. This meant that it was whirled around and pushed into towards the mainland. He had often seen logs caught like this on a piece of land, but he also knew that they often did not catch for long, and as this one wallowed in a shallow eddy by the mainland he knew that they did not have much time. He threw his body into the shallows and grabbed at the thick plant life that grew on the banks of the river. He began to heave his body up, and then he remembered the girl. She was still clinging to the wood for dear life when she should have been letting go and pushing into the shallows.

'Your arm, lift your arm!' he yelled over the sound of the rushing water. Luckily she did as she was asked and reached an arm towards him. He grabbed her hand and held on. 'Let go of the log now,' he yelled. Luckily, now that her hand was in his she obeyed his instructions and he pulled her in towards him with almost the last of his strength. 'The grasses . . . cling on to 'em,' he said, and she did as she was asked. Now that he had let go of her, he used both hands to pull his body on to the grass. His whole body ached and he longed desperately to lie on his back and gasp like a newly landed fish, but he had other business to deal with.

He got hold of the girl and pulled her up by her arms – she would have some interesting bruises later on – and made sure that she was safe before giving way to his first impulse and lying there gasping like the aforementioned piscine creature. They couldn't lie there for long, because they would grow colder than they were, and die of hypothermia. He got her to her feet and the two of them staggered towards the woodlands. Just before doing so the girl turned, water dripping from her long hair and down her slim arm as she pointed.

'Look, Ryan, look.' He followed her gaze and saw the log they had so painfully prepared for their short trip. After spending a little while wallowing at the bend of the river, it was caught by a sudden current. It was pulled away from the bank like a matchstick and swept away on the main river and around the bend towards the roaring falls, a fate that would have been theirs if they had waited a minute longer. One more thing caught his attention: further along, where the grass gave way to a sandbank, was the very boat that had brought them over. He ran to this and with a shout of fury he used some of his ebbing strength to push it into the water, where it was soon caught up in the rush and would share the fate of the log.

His cousin was not the only one who had a taste for revenge.

CHAPTER TEN

The old Camp Brazos was tucked in between the hills, but it was at a higher elevation than the surrounding land and any villages that might be nearby. Those same villages, situated as they were so close to the Mexican border, were mainly inhabited by people of the same race as those who had captured the villagers.

Things had not changed a great deal since the villagers had been herded into the compound that was to be their home – for how long they did not know. Seventy people had been torn from where they lived and thrust into captivity. As if to underline the point, three guards marched up and down the three sections of the long fence, each one carrying a rife and patrolling their own area. The rifles were rather old and looked as if they might have come from the time of the Civil War, but they had been oiled and looked as if they were functional enough. Not that any of the villagers wanted to test them out.

The gates opened and the hunting party that had been out that day returned. They brought with them a great many carcasses of animals that they had captured. The animals were piled up at the top of the courtyard, furry prospective meals. Most of the captured were turkeys, rabbits, and quail, quite a few of those, but there were three much larger kills in the form of deer, and even a wild hog with a fierce pair of tusks. It was an undeniable truth that this many people would need to be fed and that would have been the situation in the days when the camp was used for prisoners of war. Besides the animals they had brought back, the foragers had also returned with gunnysacks full of wild plants, such as potatoes, edible green leaves and berries. Somewhere deep in the buildings at the top of the square was a kitchen block where the pile of dead creatures could be turned into something more edible.

Aguste Rivero was at the scene as his men dropped off the provender and he had a satisfied smile on his face. 'Raul, Pell, Lucas, Cesar, you have done very well,' he said, with a happy smile. 'You others, too; this will feed us all while the camp is being rebuilt.' Satisfied, his men picked up their kills and took them indoors to where they would be processed.

Rivero was not finished, though. He waited patiently and there was the rumbling of hoofs and wheels rattling across the uneven ground outside. There had once been a military road that ran down from the camp, but that had partially disintegrated and it was a far from smooth ride to the main yard. No less than three wagons were brought in, ranging from the top to almost the bottom of the courtyard. The wagons were filled to the brim with building materials: stones, sacks of lime and sand, and other materials that could be used for making walls. What is more, it was clear that these could not have been loaded that morning because they held too much in the way of materials – each team of four horses pulling the wagons had been straining at their restraints just to pull them in. Now the animals were standing there panting, the sweat rolling off them.

'Put the wagons into the empty compound,' ordered Rivero, who seemed a person who liked to be in the middle of the action. His second-in-command, Ramirez, appeared at this point and the two men gave shouted orders until the wagons were safely stored a little way from each other away from the main area, but with their loads still intact. It was a process that was watched with horrified interest by the prisoners at the other side of the camp behind their fence. They instinctively knew that whatever was going on was not great news for them. This was confirmed shortly after Rivero saw the horses being led away to be fed with whatever the stables provided. He strutted up and down the fences and spoke in a clear but not particularly loud voice. However, they were all able to get his message.

'You've been here for long enough, you gringos, lazing around and living on my good will. That time is fast coming to an end. You will be coming out shortly and repairing these walls and the side buildings. You will be doing this for a reason: not just our protection, but also yours.'

'You won't get away with this,' yelled a man called Lutz from inside the compound. He had been one of the owners of the saloon. 'They'll come and get you, you an'' your murderers.' His voice was hoarse with anger. Bert, who had been standing near him, shuffled away from the protester to a different part of the compound.

'Shut up, you diseased son of a pig whore,' said Ramirez, a trace of asperity in his tone.

'He has a right to speak,' said Rivero, more mildly. 'Come forward to the fence, my friend. You have a point of view: please, come forward, tell me what you think.' Lutz looked around for support and discovered that, in a sense, he was being encouraged.

Many of the formerly apathetic villagers were looking at him. He was a big, red-faced man who looked as if he had a habit of imbibing the ale that he had sold in the saloon. He drew strength from the many eyes on him, but Bert, speaking in a low voice, came out with a warning. 'Don't do this, Pere. Don't do it.'

Lutz ignored this and went over to the fence, feeling the strength of those behind him. He faced Rivero, who was looking faintly amused, and Ramirez, who was looking the exact opposite. Ramirez looked as if he wanted to speak again, but his commander was keeping him silent with a warning look.

'We are free Americans,' said Lutz. 'My parents came from Germany when I was a small child. I grew up here, this is my country and these are my people. We have rights, do you understand? Rights. I was dragooned here and in shock. Now the shock has gone and I must stand up for these people.'

'You make the valid points,' said Rivero. 'Your protest is noted. Now be quiet and do your work with the rest – you are all going to rebuild what is to be your home for

74

the duration.'

'They will come,' said Lutz. 'Don't you understand? They will come, and when they do, you and your kind will be destroyed.'

'Yes, they will come,' said Rivero, 'and that is the reason why you all have to set to work. But who is it that will arrive to rescue you? A group of cowboys, that is who, for that is who is left in that area. Cowboys.' His companion, Ramirez, gave a laugh at this and spat on the ground, indicating what he at least thought of ranch riders.

'The government will find out about this outrage,' said Lutz. 'You will be overturned by the military.'

'You are right,' said Rivero regretfully, 'that is what will happen, but by that time we will be strong enough to resist them, and we have our prisoners as a bargaining tool, of course.'

'You're all going to die!' screamed Lutz, suddenly losing all self-control and rattling the rusty but still strong bars of the fence.

'Ah, up until now I thought you would be a reasonable man,' said Rivero. 'Look at this, all of you! This is what this man has brought on his own head.' Too late, Lutz realized what he had done, and why he should not have protested. He turned to run away from the leader, but as he did so Rivero took a gun from a beautifully fashioned leather holster, and fired once, but hardly able to miss at such a short range. There was a bang that sounded almost subdued in that open space, and the former saloonkeeper received a wound from the bullet that was immediately fatal. The dead man fell instantly, his corpse

75

lying on the ground, looking up with unseeing eyes.

This calm act said more to the villagers than any amount of shouting, screaming or expostulating from the rebel leader might have done. Two of the women there began to scream and moan in horror and some of the men shouted in protest at the outrage, quickly quelled by a sharp word from Ramirez.

'Now, get the guards, open the gates and start them working,' said Rivero to his lieutenant. 'As for that,' he pointed to the corpse, 'feed it to the dogs. We waste nothing.' Then he marched off back to his headquarters, a busy man who wanted to get things done.

CHAPTER ELEVEN

'What's your name? I know your face from when you were younger,' Jay asked the young man who stood beside McArthur. 'I need to know, because the sheriff'll need to know who he's hanging.'

'I'm Jardine,' gabbled the young man, 'Mack Jardine.' He looked very young and almost as if he was going to burst into tears. Scott glared at him.

'Shoulda kept that gab of yours sealed,' he said.

'I say we keep it simple,' said Clay. 'Let's hang 'em here and now to save a lot of trouble.'

'I won't tell you where he is,' said McArthur. 'You'll never know, and he'll be dead pretty quickly.' He looked straight at his uncle when he said this. Hawk managed to restrain the degree of anger that told him he should shoot McArthur straight in the face. Besides, it wasn't as simple as that: McArthur was family, and Hawk valued his relationships even with those who were supposedly a lost cause. 'I guess I don't need to ask you much,' said Hawk. 'Yancey, you're not the most clever of men, and I think you listened to the fairy tales from these two and thought

77

that they were going to make you rich. Well, I can help you here. I've got money with me. I'll give you five hundred dollars if you tell me where my boy's been imprisoned.'

'Don't say a word, Yancey,' said Scott in a sandpaper rough tone. Yancey stood there, frozen by uncertainty. 'He's lying; he'll give you the money, all right, then he'll turn you over to the law.'

'You'll turn me in,' said Yancey hoarsely, 'but I'll die first.'

'Right, men, guard those two. I'll deal with this one. Come on, Yancey, you and me, we're going for a little walk.' Hawk brandished his weapon, and now that his rage had somewhat deflated, Yancey – who was as reluctant as anyone to receive a bullet in the head – obeyed. The pair of them walked to the edge of the woodland where the horses were tethered, and Hawk went over to his own animal, reaching into the saddle-bag with one hand while continuing to hold his gun on the large man with the other. Luckily, and he knew this, one of the bundles of notes contained exactly 500 dollars. Being a neat man, as he saved money he tended to bundle it in exact sums. The bundle of notes was held together by twine. 'I know that they influenced you, Yancey, and you're really a good guy.' He threw the bundle of notes to the big man. 'Here, count these, and take my word for it: if you help me get my boy back, I'll make sure you keep the money.' Yancey stared at the bundle of notes in his big hands. It was more money than he had ever seen in his life at a time when even when he was in full employment he would earn about thirty dollars a month.

His mouth worked, and for the first time since they had met again, he seemed humbled.

'Your boy means this much to you, don't he? I can't take this.' He looked straight at Hawk. 'I done wrong, didn't I, real wrong? Your boy's on Shrine Island, that's where he is, along with the girl.'

'Girl, what girl?'

'They had a girl. She was real quiet; never knew her name.' He handed the money back to Hawk, hanging his head. Hawk took the bundle off him but looked directly at the large man. 'I'll keep these dollars, but you'll get them if you lead me to my boy.' He lowered his gun. 'Are we together on this one?'

There was a strange look in Yancey's eyes as he looked at Hawk. 'You'll do that? You'll help me?'

'I keep my word,' said Hawk, 'and we have to do this now. Who knows what kind of trouble he is in?' Together they went to the woodland where Clay, Holt and Flynn were patiently guarding their prisoners. 'Right, men, could you follow me? Bring those two with you.'

'Aw, they're a pain,' said Holt. 'Can't we just shoot 'em?'

'I told you, no shooting anyone in cold blood,' said Hawk. 'Just make sure they don't escape.' Together the men walked towards the source of the roaring sound that they could all hear. Hawk knew Shrine Island quite well, given that it was a sacred place to some of his ancestors. The walk to the river was a sombre one. Hawk took the lead with Yancey walking beside him, and he was not holding a gun in sight.

'Club him, Yancey,' said Scott in a chilling voice. 'You

do that, the three of us has got a chance. . . .' But Yancey walked on as if he had not heard, keeping pace with Hawk who traversed the rough woodland with practised ease.

His men were not so sure; they were riders, not walkers, and they often stumbled on tree roots or thick vegetation, which meant that there was a very real danger that their prisoners might take a chance and elude them. However, when Clay stumbled right behind Scott, Hawk heard the hesitation in his employee's stride and turned back instantly, drawing out his gun and covering Scott until Clay recovered. Scott had played in these woodlands when he was young and he knew how easy it was to get lost in the thick growths around them, and once that happened to him his captors would probably never see him again.

'Someone's had a fire around here,' said Hawk almost conversationally. 'The smoke has drifted through the trees. I hope it's not Indians. If it is I'll have to pow-wow with them.' None of his men had noticed the wood smoke, but they were not attuned to the woodlands the way he was.

Then they were down at the banks of the river, Hawk's uncanny sense of place having led him to the exact spot where they would face Shrine Island. It was getting late in the day by then, and the rushing waters that foamed as they travelled around the bend of the river and down the falls were a daunting sight.

'The boat they used is real near,' said Yancey. 'Used it to cross the foamy way.' He led them along to the sandbar, his eyes bulging in his broad face as he looked at the space where the craft had been. 'Leastways it was here.' He looked around helplessly like a man who has seen a magic trick and doesn't know how it was done. Hawk, however, was more astute and examined the sand.

'I can see where the boat has been dragged along and cast off,' he said, straightening up. He looked directly at his nephew. 'What do you know about this?'

However, Scott was staring off into the middle distance. 'Don't know, don't care,' he said. 'Just throw me in the river, let me die on the falls, bash my brains out on the rocks below.' And as he said these words there was a rustle of undergrowth and a fury rushed forward, club in hand, and attacked him, so that it looked as if his wish was about to be granted with wood instead of water.

When the young man and his companion went back into the woodlands after setting the boat adrift – and watching it sweep away to an inevitable doom – Ryan had taken the girl to one of the many clearings created by fallen trees, and he did not hesitate in what he had to do. He gathered some dry grass, of which there was plenty, struck some stones against metal and was able to create a spark that ignited the grass. Then, with the help of the girl, he fed the resulting flame with dry twigs, and eventually branches, until they had a fair sized fire. He was careful to use a splayed branch like a type of makeshift brush and swept the area around the fire, creating a bare space so that the flames did not spread much further. This was a vital thing to do because they did not want to create a woodland fire. He had seen such things before, caused by careless cowboys, and they were not a pretty sight and one would probably kill them.

Ryan was a plainsman, but he knew that the wood-lands around them were so heavy because they were fed by the rich soil that accumulated around any huge river, and the Brazos brought down a lot of nutrients from the hills that enabled the vegetation to proliferate.

They had been cold and hardly able to move when they started, but the work and resulting heat of the fire had warmed their limbs and stopped the possibility of the pair dying from hypothermia.

'We'll stay here for as short a time as possible,' said Ryan. 'Who knows when they'll come back to check on us?'

'That's right.' The girl gave a shiver. She was no longer cold, so lack of warmth could not have been the reason. 'You don't know what they were like with me, you don't know.'

Once more Ryan felt a strange kind of shyness come over him. Despite his leaning towards book learning, he was not wise in the ways of the world. 'Tell me what they did.' He waited but no answer came.

The girl was leaning into the flames and for a moment he thought she was going to put one of her hands in the fire. Then she picked up one of the branches about as thick as the arm of a man and fed the flames again. She did not answer him and the look on her face warned him not to speak about the subject again.

'Once we're warmed up we'll go back to the ranch,' said Ryan at last. 'It's a fair walk, but if we make a good pace we'll be there within the hour.'

Then there came the sound that they had dreaded.

The woodlands were a place in which man rarely intruded and they could hear the sound of people crashing down what trail there was with all the subtlety of a herd of elephants. The thing was, it sounded like more than before.

Ryan hastily took up his makeshift brush – the branch with spreading twigs – and hastened to brush bare earth onto the fire to douse any smoke and flames. It had done its job and saved their lives.

The girl stood up ready for flight like a startled deer.

Ryan's expression became grim. 'If it's them, we wait in hiding and get them. If we try to flee they might chase after and kill us with their guns; at least this way we'll be fighting back.'

The girl said nothing but gave a brief nod of her fair head to show that she was with him in this. They took up branches that had once been destined for the fire but were tapered and easy to hold in the hand and a good approximation of clubs.

'They're heading for the river,' she said.

'That's not a surprise,' said Ryan, 'which means they've either got their ransom or they're going to check on us.' He spoke in as low a voice as possible, and once they heard the sound of the footsteps going away from them they followed after, heading for the very sandbar from which they had cast off the boat.

They peered out from the undergrowth and Ryan felt his heart give an unexpected leap of delight when he saw his father and fellow workers. The prisoners, he saw, were the very men who had taken them captive, and from the expression on their faces he knew they were under duress.

He was just debating the best way to approach them without being fired upon when the girl gave a grunt not suited to her good looks and ran forward, thrusting out the club and attacking McArthur.

She managed to get a few good blows on his head and body before she was restrained by the men around her. Hawk had the presence of mind to grab the makeshift club off her and throw it away. Scott said nothing in protest, mostly because she had knocked him unconscious. He was bleeding at the temples, and it was clear that if she had used metal instead of wood his skull would have been broken.

Clay and Holt were holding the girl back and she was struggling with them, her breathing shortening and the panic arising in her of what they were going to do to her.

Hawk saw the fear in her eyes. 'If they let you go, will you refrain from attacking anyone else?' he asked reasonably enough. She gave a brief nod at this and they let her go. She stood in front of them, breathing heavily and staring at Yancey.

'What's he doing with you? Tie him up, he's a kidnapper.'

At that moment Ryan stepped from the woodlands. Father and son looked at each other.

'Hello, son,' said Hawk.

CHAPTER TWELVE

Not much was said as the prisoners were brought back to the ranch, the Lazy H. Hawk wore an air of quiet relief, but there was no triumph and no victory in gaining back that which had been his in the first place – the company of his son. Anyway, Ryan had taken no small part in his own rescue and his own survival.

By the time they got back to the ranch it was starting to grow dark and there was a chill in the air. The cattle were still out in the meadows around the ranch, but it was spring and the grass was growing well, and the land was interlaced with streams of ice-cold water that came off the hills. They could and would survive without the attentions of man for a good long time. Their prisoners were all conscious by this time because Scott had revived on the long journey, flung as he was across the saddle of a horse. He had struggled to escape, but his hands were bound and he was unable to do so. He had shouted many imprecations, calling Hawk names that the latter had heard many times in his life, but his uncle was unmoved.

Being called a half-breed bastard did not affect his mind at all.

What happened next was a different matter altogether. They stopped at the fence around the ranch and had a short discussion of what they were going to do with the prisoners.

'Throw 'em in the barn all tied up,' said Clay, 'then we can take 'em to the law tomorrow.'

'That sounds about right,' said Hawk. 'There's the tricky proposition of what to do with you, Yancey. You won't be swayed by these here reprobates again, will you?' The big, thickset man frowned, looking at the ground, a bemused expression on his strangely smooth face.

'I guess those buttheads will try and sway me, Indian man.'

'You see,' Hawk turned to his men, 'you must keep them in the bunkhouse. There's plenty of room, and a pot-bellied stove to heat the place up. We'll do just as Clay says and deal with them early on the morrow. You can do that just now, men. I would thank you for that. I need to speak to Rye alone.'

'What about me?' demanded the girl. 'Where am I to go?'

'Just walk over to the side of the ranch,' said Hawk. 'What I have to say to my son will take one minute.' The men were already leading the prisoners to the bluff that hid the bunkhouse, and the girl followed, but only as far as the side of the hill. She looked at them thoughtfully from the distance.

'What is it that you couldn't tell me in front of them?'

86

asked Ryan. 'We must hurry; I want to see Mom. Did you get Martha in to look after her?' Martha was a domestic from the village who had been coming in to help them from time to time during his mother's illness.

'That's what I wanted to tell you, son. I'm afraid your mother is gone.'

'Away? To the village? How?'

Hawk did not have to say anything else; his dark eyes bore into those of his only surviving child.

'No! Was it them? Did they go in and kill her when they took me?' A cry of outrage was sharp and torn deep from inside.

'Son, your mom was on the edge of existence for long enough; she was ready to go and meet her maker. That was the truth of the matter, and I made sure she knew nothing about the kidnap. She died with a blessing on her lips for your future.'

'Where is she? Is she there? Can I see her for one last time?'

'Come with me and I'll show you.' Hawk gave a nod to the girl to follow them, but she could see that there was some traumatic exchange going on between the two men and kept a respectful distance. Hawk led his son to the back of the ranch and down the slope to the elder tree that guarded the graves of their relatives. Ryan walked forward, his lips trembling and fell to his knees when he saw the newly dug grave. He spoke a few low words that even Hawk, who was standing by his side, could not hear, then stood up, turned and did something he would never have contemplated in his normal life: he dug his hand deep in the pocket of his father's coat and

87

snatched out one of his guns. His face was a bloodless mask in the gathering twilight and he strode away from the graveyard and the mortal remains of his mother with a look on his face that denoted ill for anyone who got in his way.

He managed by dint of his long legs and athletic stride, and a newfound energy that had been ebbing away during the long climb to the ranch. It was an energy that was directed to one course only: he was going to get his cousin.

The three men who had kidnapped him were standing before the bunkhouse, now being urged inside by Holt and Clay, both of who had guns. Ryan ran forward with his gun at the ready and Scott turned just as the avenging figure appeared. Ryan went straight up to him, a strange calmness coming over him as he put the gun to the forehead of the man he intended to kill.

Scott opened his lips, but nothing came from his throat but a wordless croak. He was experiencing the last few seconds of his worthless life and he could say nothing. Just as Ryan was tightening his finger on the trigger there was a thump on his shoulder and the gun jerked to one side, there was a roar as it came into action and the bullet buried itself in the wooden wall of the bunkhouse.

Ryan turned with a shout of rage and raised the gun again, only to find that he was pointing it at the head of his own father. Not fast enough to catch up with his boy, Hawk had lobbed a rock at him that had hit him on the shoulder.

'Drop the weapon,' said Hawk. 'Blood demands

blood, I know that. But you're wrong this time.' For a moment – more like a fleeting second – it looked as if the bloodlust had not ended and Ryan was going to fire on his own father, but the rage in his eyes died and he allowed the gun to thud to the ground where it was picked up hastily by Clay.

'Give that gun to me!' yelled the girl, rushing forward with an almost demonic expression on her normally pretty features. 'He deserves it from me. I'll blow out his worthless brains.' Such was her fury and determination that for a second it looked as if she was going to succeed in wresting the weapon from Clay, the man who had picked it up just a second before. This time, paradoxically, it was Ryan who pulled her away from the prisoners.

Jardine was looking shell-shocked by the whole thing, but it was Scott who looked at them with a certain determination. 'Know what? If that's goin' to be the way of it, end it now and save me from the rope, 'cause it looks as if that's the way it's going anyway. Nobody ever gave me anything, and when I try to get somethin', I get this.'

'You shut up,' said Clay roughly, and forced the younger, slimmer man inside the bunkhouse. Yancey, although they were keeping an eye on him, went inside of his own free will, followed by Jardine who was guarded by Holt.

Hawk looked at his son and the young girl. 'Time we got some rest,' he said, turning as he did so, and after a moment's hesitation they followed after.

A day can pass in what seems like a moment, or it can take forever. To the new inhabitants of Camp Brazos they had experienced the latter sensation. Rivero was soon able to set up a division of labour that suited his purposes. The children – even those who were barely able to walk – were set to the task of mixing the materials that created the mortar for the walls. The women were given the task of unloading the bricks and stones from the carts that would form the body of the repairs. The men, because they were physically stronger than the women, were given the task of laying the bricks and mortar. In all cases they were supervised by guards with quirts, and the guards had orders to use these if the workers flagged.

However, after several hours of this, which by necessity had involved some sort of training in each task, Rivero got a bugler to sound the call and the work came to a halt. The prisoners, although they were hardly a threat by now, were herded back into their compound.

'Rest and drink water. Food will be with you soon,' said Rivero as he marched up and down the parade ground. 'Do not think I am being merciful when I let you rest; you are just tools for my task.' The food distributed to them – thrown through the fence by some bored-looking men – was fairly basic anyway: scraps of meat and unleavened bread that looked as if it had been baked on flat griddles. The people in the compound were left to decide how they were going to divide the food amongst themselves, but once more it was Bert and Aimee who showed some sort of natural leadership.

'We do this fairly,' he said. 'Gather up what's here and set it out, and all have a share. If we act like animals and scrabble about and demand more than we need each, even though there's not enough for all of us, they'll have won.'

Aimee helped him gather the food, and the people, who were desperate for some sense of normality, gave in to their forceful personalities. The food was divided up as mentioned, although one young woman barely took anything. She was about seventeen years old and would have been good-looking if it had not been for the dust that marred her features. Her plain black dress was stained, too, for none of them were dressed in what could have been called working clothes.

'Lena, you have to eat,' scolded Aimee. Lena had been her maid when she was running the boarding house what seemed like a thousand years ago.

'I thought he would come for me,' she said.

'Who?'

'Ryan. He was my special friend, but he's like all the rest: he's abandoned us. What's the use of food? That'll just give us more strength so they can work us to death.' She nibbled at some of the flatbread and took a draught of water from one of the earthen jugs that had been provided. They were all drinking a lot of water due to the dusty work.

'Now look, my girl, just because some rancher's boy has been mooning over you, it don't mean that he's abandoned you. There must be some rescue effort that's afoot. They can't just barge in, you know, that would be suicide. These men are armed to the teeth, and by the way they act and all the animals they've killed, they're pretty good at what they do.'

'Then maybe he'll come?'

91

'You'll need a lot more than an eighteen-year-old boy to get you out of this, but yes, he could still come here.' There was a rattling on the bars as some of the so-called soldiers walked up and down with sticks and battered away at the metal. Ramirez stood there. He was dressed in black and wearing long boots and cradling a Winchester '73 in his arms. It was clear that the Mexicans did not think all things produced by the Americans were bad. Some of the prisoners looked up like startled deer while others lifted their heads in a listless manner.

'Get back to work,' said Ramirez, unlocking one of the gates and allowing the prisoners to come out in three and fours so that they were unable to get together and rush any of the guards. As they emerged, they were led away to their specific work parties according to their sex and size. As Bert (who was not able to climb their ladders because of his weight) passed the second-in-command, he gave Ramirez a silent glare that said everything about his feelings. 'Eyes on the task, gringo,' said the lieutenant, and shoved Bert in the back. The overweight man stumbled and nearly fell but continued onwards with a murderous look in his eyes.

A young girl came out of the compound with a bewildered look in her eyes and Ramirez looked at her with a faint leer on his unshaven features. She shrank away from him.

Their lot could get worse, a lot worse.

CHAPTER THIRTEEN

Hawk arose early the next morning, but he was not up as early as his son. He found Ryan down at the family plot beside his mother's grave. He was kneeling on the ground when his father arrived, his head bowed, but somehow Hawk thought that he had not really been praying for his mother's soul. There was a brooding intensity about the young man that said that he had not yet come to terms with what had happened. Hawk stood near him for what seemed like hours but was in reality only a few minutes until, at last, the young man stood up and waited beside his father. They were not the kind of people who showed their emotions to each other but Hawk put out his hand and squeezed his son's arm, nodded once, and began to walk away. His son followed.

Back at the ranch the young woman, Abbey, had pre-pared them a simple breakfast consisting of eggs, bacon and beans. It was the kind of meal that saw them through the day when they were going about their normal business. They thanked her and ate in comparative silence. The girl had found some female garments that had been long unused, in storage, and with Hawk's tacit consent she had changed into these. They were from before his wife had become unwell, and fitted the girl well because Mary had been a slim woman with a lot of nervous energy who had never kept still.

'Time to go into town and jail them prisoners,' said Hawk. 'Although might be better to get a coach and take 'em to the nearest town.'

'They sure can't stay here,' agreed Ryan, 'I would kill 'em if they did, simple as that, what he did to me – and you,' he said, looking at the girl. She flushed and looked down at her plate.

'Blow his brains out,' she said. 'Jardine's too. They're worthless, the pair of them. Yancey is just a big lug who did what he was told because he thought it was easy money, but you should jail him too; they couldn't have done it without him.'

'Time to go,' said Hawk, not a man who enjoyed getting into arguments.

The prisoners had been fed, too, and there was an air of sullen resignation about them as Holt and Clay hitched a team of horses to a flat wagon, tied their hands and legs, and threw them inside. It was still early in the day and Hawk rode beside Ryan, who had slept like one dead the previous night, as had the girl in the spare room. There had been not a lot of time to explain the circumstances of what they were about to see and now he was taking the opportunity to give his son the information he would

94

need to make sense of the situation.

'Although we're jailing 'em, to get 'em away from us, Clay or Holt or Flynn – whichever one wants to do his duty – might have to act as a temporary lawmaker. The other ranchers will swear him in. The entire population of the village who could travel on two feet are gone, taken by bandits the night before last.'

'Why didn't you tell me sooner?'

'Well, you had a lot on your plate, what with your mother and all.'

'Where have they taken the people?'

'That's the problem: nobody knows.'

Ryan said nothing but there was a return of the brooding darkness that had been around him since his kidnap.

When they arrived in the village, the rancher Hawk had met the previous day was still there. It looked as if he was living in one of the two-dozen buildings scattered around: certainly he had his choice of accommodation. He came out and greeted the newcomers as the cart rumbled to a stop.

'What's going on?'

'Not much,' admitted Lamington. 'The other ranchers – I've left my spread in the care of my brood and I'm minding the store, so to speak – but they're away making plans, so they say, to track down these here bandits.'

'They've had days,' said Hawk bluntly. 'A posse should have been formed by now. They should have tracked down these evil raiders.'

'Ain't quite that easy,' said Lamington. 'This ain't some bunch of bank robbers who made off with a week's takings. This is a highly organised private army with some point to prove, leastways that's what I made out from the account of old Betsy.'

'Betsy who?'

'Betsy Ross, grandma of the storekeeper, lives on the second floor and she's bedridden, she hasn't been out for years. Crawled to her window and saw the whole thing.'

'Is she still around?'

'I've been tending to her and one or two others who were sick or crippled and couldn't be taken. She'll tell you the whole thing.'

While they had been discussing the matter the cart had been emptied of its occupants, who were being led towards the only jail in Hatton Falls, a building on its own with bars in the windows that had been tended by the owner of the hardware store, Jake Giles. He was the only titular lawman round here, but he was now one of the abducted.

'Guess you'll have to go in there too and ride shotgun on these two, Yancey,' said Holt, who was a little more officious than his fellow riders, 'being as you was involved in the whole thing.'

'Mayhap a restin' would be good. Yum, yum, three big meals a day too,' said the big man, who seemed quite struck by the idea. 'Maybe see Bert too, cousin to me.' The riders looked at each other. This was information they had not known, and perhaps the reason why Yancey had landed up in Hatton Falls in the first place.

'They're going to hang you too,' said Scott dourly. 'That's the reason they're putting you in with us.' Clay gave the prisoner a swift smack in the face.

'Shut up, scum-sucking mollusc. You speak when

you're spoken to.' The three men were led inside, with Yancey still cogitating over the matter.

In the meantime, Hawk was looking at the burned saloon with a thoughtful look on his face.

'So, what have the scouts told you?' he asked Lamington.

'Scouts?'

'One of the basic ways of getting the information you need: you send out scouts and you get on the trail of the parties who did this to get some of the information you need for the attack. My father did it all the time during the Civil War. His kind were invaluable for the cause.'

'I – I guess I don't know,' said Lamington. 'As I say, I'm minding the store, so to speak, and looking after the sick and old along with a couple of folks from the ranches, but no one had told me anything to do with scouts.'

In the meantime, now that he had seen his enemies, as he considered them, safely ensconced in the prison, Ryan was finishing his tour of the village. The shock on his face when he saw the burnt-out remains of the saloon was still a little visible, but it was overlaid by sadness at the discovery that the girl he had known so well, Lena, was counted as one of the missing. It was his turn to approach the man who was minding Hatton Falls.

'Where is she?'

The rancher looked at him with some bemusement. 'Who?'

'Lena Zweig. She was the maid for Aimee Struthers, who ran the cowboy boarding house. The one that gets real busy during the cattle drives.'

'They must have took her, son; certainly no one by

that name around here now I would've known.'

Ryan turned and looked at his father with an expression on his face that said more than any words.

Hawk had nothing to lose. He looked back at Ryan, and Abbey, who was standing beside him, then turned to Lamington. 'Joe, there ain't a party on the go as far as you know it?'

'I guess what they're doing is making plans and hoping to send out a whole bunch of men at one time, that way they hope to overwhelm whoever's done this. Leastways that was the idea they chewed over last time they was here.'

Hawk could understand why the village would be a good meeting point for the ranchers. Between them they commanded hundreds of miles of land, and meeting up at one ranch or another would be a difficult task, while the village was a central point where they could all gather. 'When are they coming around again?'

'Tonight, from what I could gather; they're making sure all that's there is secure.'

'So if they meet tonight, the soonest they'll get something done is tomorrow even if they set off early?'

'I guess so.'

'It's not good enough,' said Hawk. 'It's already been a couple of days and those prisoners could be undergoing anything at the moment – torture and murder of all kinds.'

'Lena,' said Ryan, as if the word had been torn from him, 'she's only a young girl. They could be doing anything they want.'

His expression was one of cold fury. 'I'm going to kill

them, kill them all.'

'Ryan, don't do it,' said Abbey suddenly and with a passion that surprised him. 'From what I hear they're heavily armed, and they don't care, whoever they are. They'll kill you, and the rest of us. For all you know the girl might already be dead. There's nothing you can do for her, nothing.' So great was her passion as she said this that she looked briefly into his suddenly stony features, then stamped away, hand to her face.

'What's got into her?' asked Ryan, strangely disconcerted by the fact that his father was bearing a faint smile on his normally inscrutable features.

Hawk soon lost his smile as he looked back at Lamington. 'What we need to do is send in a party of men who will find out what is going on. When that's done, they'll come back and the real work can begin. But such a party would have to be well-stocked and well-armed and ready for whatever is directed against them.'

'It's early spring,' said Lamington, 'an' it was a bad winter, real rainy, and snow too, although luckily they missed most of that down here beside the river; the water melted most of the snow and raised the temperatures. But it means that most of the ranchers are getting their longhorns out to fresh pasture. There's a lot of work going on an' they're rounding up the strays, too. There are not as many cowboys out here either; they come in during the cattle drives, so there's just not as many people around. We're all mustering our forces but it takes that bit of time, and we're all outraged and arming up to take on these vile brigands.' He spoke with real fire in his eyes and in a tone that was outraged at the implication that nothing was being done for those who had been affected by the scurrilous invasion and abduction of their people.

'Then a body of riders needs to be found fast,' said Hawk, 'and I know who they are.'

CHAPTER FOURTEEN

In any enterprise it is amazing how sheer hard work can lead to the desired result. The walls of Camp Brazos had gone to ruin mostly in the middle, where they had crumbled downwards due to many years of neglect and the sometimes severe winters that occurred around here, but the base had been solidly built on strong foundations, and the corners had been strengthened where they were adjoined by thick adobe below and double brickwork above. Clearly those who had designed the prison had decided that they were there for the duration of the Civil War, no matter how long it took. This meant that by concentrating on the centre of the walls, repairs were soon effected that made it look more like it would have been some twenty years before.

Clearly the cost of maintaining an unused building – or rather series of buildings – was such that the government had abandoned it due to a lack of prisoners, since the war had ended in defeat for the seven Confederate forces – the state of Texas amongst them – who had tried to secede from the USA and declare themselves a separate nation.

It was now the end of the third day of building, and Aguste Rivero walked in the muted sunshine as the hills around them cast their long shadows on the prison. Several men had died during the night, exhausted as they were by the constant work schedule and the low amount of food that they had consumed. Ramirez, who seemed to take on the day-to-day mundane tasks of running the camp, had immediately ordered some of his men to take away the bodies.

'And do not just dump them in the woods or throw them in the river anymore,' he had instructed. 'Bury them, even if in the shallowest of graves.' The bodies had been thrown into one of the now empty carts and transported away by men who grumbled at their task. There was a reason for his caution: bodies seen floating in the river would be visible to the inevitable pursuers, and cause an urgent attack that might well be dispelled by a simple act.

Rivero watched the cart rumble through the restored gates that had been fortified with strips of iron and gave a little shrug. The price was small and not worth thinking about. The new walls rose around them, and were already solidly in place.

'You have used the prisoners well and done a good job, Raul,' he said to his second-in-command. 'I would not have believed the task could have been done so swiftly if it had not been with my own eyes.'

'These gringos, dare I say it, can toil hard when they are pushed,' said Ramirez. 'The gun and the knife have been sufficient threat, although I did have to beat one or two to get the best result out of them.'

Rivero walked the length of the parade ground. The compound on the far side of the camp, opposite the one where the prisoners were kept, had been the most ruinous. It backed on to the hills above and would have been the weakest point for their defences if it had not been repaired. The way the walls had been constructed was such that they widened at the top and there was a guard tower in each corner. The guard towers were roofed over by little porticos so that the inhabitant was well sheltered, with an all-round view of the camp and the surrounding area. These had been ruined, too, but had also been restored. They were reached by the guard slinging his weapon over his back and climbing up using metal rungs set in the walls. These freshly restored shelters high above were already inhabited by his soldiers.

'This is what I had pictured when I came here with you all those months ago,' said Rivero, 'a place in which our own private army could form an enclave, with an assurance that they could defend it from those who would come here.'

'What I still do not understand is why you would use the gringos when there are any number of peasant villages across the water? We could have brought them here, hundreds if you had wanted, restored the camp, then shot as many as we wanted without the Americans even knowing.'

'Ah, Raul, you are of noble blood and you look on the peasantry as mere fodder for whatever task you want. This is not about labour, not really, although the restoration of the Brazos camp was urgent. What this is about is striking back.'

'You are an idealist, Aguste.'

'There have to be such people in the world. I own this land; there is no doubt about that. My family were forced off these hills less than sixty years ago. To the Americans might is right, and the reason I used their own people is to show that we can strike back when we want and take back what is ours.'

Ramirez digested these words for a little while. 'But I thought the purpose of this strike was to get the gold and silver that is stockpiled in these very hills?'

'The White Mine? Yes, that is where we are going, so soon that I can almost see the darkness before me. From there we will get the gold that has been left there by my ancestors for the picking. They were wise, you see, they mined the area then hid stocks so that they could go back and get the gold when the value was high. It is hidden behind rocky enclaves deep in the mine.'

'Our version of El Dorado,' breathed Ramirez with a far away look in his eyes, 'except it is as real as these walls around us.'

'As for the prisoners, if they thought building these walls was a task, wait until they have to go down the mines; they will soon find out what work is.'

'But I still don't understand why you took Americans.'

'Don't you see? I have spread it far and wide that we have done this purely as a political act to get our lands

104

back. The land does not bother me as much as you think, but the gold does. Once we have mined these hills we will go back to what is now Mexico and live our lives better than any Hispaniola Grandee, and ultimately I may even be able to buy myself into a presidency.' Rivero's voice trailed off as he realized that he had said too much. 'Feed them, give them water, and celebrate with our men tonight,' he added. 'Give the men wine and meat, and let them take the women they want from the filthy gringos. I myself would not touch them, but when the celebrations have ended, on the morrow we shall take to the hills and open the mines that will make us millions.'

Ryan stared at his father with an expression that quickly became stony. 'I don't think that's a good idea at all, Father, not a good idea at all.'

'Offering a chance is always a good idea,' said his Hawk with an equally stony look on his face. 'Those people are suffering; who knows what has happened to them by now.'

The two men were still in Hatton Falls, since there did not seem to be much point going back to the ranch. Most of the work at this time of year had to do with rounding up cattle and making sure that they did not stray too far from the land, or checking that the ones due to calve were healthy enough, and most of the time they were. They were standing outside the only secure building in town, the prison. His men had established makeshift homes in the eerily empty houses up and down the main street. Hawk called them out to stand in front of him like a motley army, no two dressed alike.

Lamington, seeing that they had decided to stay for at least a couple of days, had ridden out of town to go back to his own family.

'Alonzo, Frank, Logan . . . you have all been good guys as far as I'm concerned. You've done your work well and you've proven that you are men of worth. I'm going after these bastards.'

'Me too,' said Ryan.

'As I was saying, I'm going after these bastards, and I'm going to do what every good scout does: I'm going to test the lie of the land. If there's anything I can do, I'll do it. But right now I'm going to ask the three of you if you'll come with me. There may be trouble and none of you signed up for that, but we have to show these people that we ain't going to take this kind of humiliation.'

'Or we could get the Texas Rangers,' said Holt, 'just saying.'

'Does that mean you're out then?' asked Hawk. 'Sure, if it was easy as that I'd say the same thing, but this far out, in what's still pioneer country, the Rangers will take days to contact. Hell, we ain't got the telegraph system yet.'

'Well you're wrong,' said Holt, 'if you're in, I'm in, Hawk.' The other two said nothing but looked at the man who had brought them into his business all those years ago, who had always been tough but fair with them, and merely gave a slight inclination of their heads to show their full agreement.

'Tell them the next part,' said Ryan.

'Yep, well this is the part you guys might have difficulty digesting,' said Hawk. 'I propose we take Scott, Mack and

Yancey with us.'

At these words the three men started to speak at once, making it clear what they thought of the idea. Hawk waited patiently until they stopped what they were saying.

'I understand your objections, and on the face of it, it don't seem that sensible, but these are young, fit men. They know the lie of the land because they've been tooling around here looking for a way to make easy money, and best of all, they're looking for a way to save their damned necks.'

'They might just run off,' said Flynn.

'We'll make sure we don't give them a chance,' said Hawk.

'They might turn on us,' said Holt.

'We'll make sure they aren't armed unless they need to be.' He spoke to them a little more about his ideas, and grudgingly his three employees accepted. In a sense they were relieved, because Yancey had the build of a minor giant, while the presence of the younger men might deflect some of the potential trouble heading their direction.

'We go as soon as we've prepared the way,' said Hawk. 'Time to get busy.'

CHAPTER FIFTEEN

'What are you doing?' asked Abbey, as Ryan came into the hardware store. It was remarkably well equipped compared to most of its kind in small villages, but there was a reason for this: Giles Hardware had originally been one of the pioneering trading posts on the Brazos River. It was the reason – besides the flat lie of the land and plentiful game – for why there was a village here at all.

'I might have to ask you the same thing,' he said.

'Just looking,' she answered. 'I've sheltered at the boarding house for the time being. When you think of it that's the perfect place to stay: plenty of spare rooms at this time of year.'

'Sure thing,' he said, but his eyes were darting around the building. The front of the store had a counter to one side, and all sorts of goods that a traveller might need, such as handguns, shovels and panning equipment – because of the rumoured gold in the hills – along with plenty of dried and even a few tinned foods, and pickles in jars. At the back of the store was another storeroom that only Giles would access in the course of the business.

He didn't have any keys to the store and the door was locked.

' 'Scuse me,' he said to the girl. He picked up one of the handguns (a Smith & Wesson), found the necessary bullets, loaded up and pointed it at the lock. 'You want to get out?' he asked her. 'The bullets might bounce back; don't want to put you in danger.' He noticed then that she was holding a gun of her own. 'You getting some personal protection?'

'So why are you breaking in?' she asked. 'There's plenty of goods out here. More than you need.'

'Tell you later,' he said, 'but be careful with that thing: it can hurt your hand when it goes off. Now please get out.' She did not leave the building, but backed away and stood behind the counter as he fired at the lock. The sound was almost deafening in the enclosed space of the building. Ryan gave the door a kick and it fell in. There, in the back of the building, was what he was looking for. Giles stocked barrels of gunpowder. These were not the huge ones used by the army or industrialists, but individual kegs about the size of a man's head. Altogether there were a dozen of these, along with rifles, a small cannon and even cannon balls made of solid iron. These were deceptively small, but when lifted weighed pounds, and were capable of doing a great deal of damage.

'You were risking it shooting into the door,' said the girl, coming forward.

'Not really,' he said, 'the kegs are shelved higher up and a bullet ain't going to make much difference to an iron cannon.' He left her behind and went to the front of the building. 'Guys, I've found what we need. Get the cart ready.' Hawk entered the building and gave the girl a nod. By this time she had acquired a bag, a feminine one that she had obviously taken from the boarding house, and the gun was gone. He took it she was there looking for food, which she was, too.

'Hey,' Hawk stood and looked at the twenty or so kegs and gave a low whistle. 'It's a lot more impressive when you see 'em in a row like this.' Ryan was standing there with an air of a proprietor's pride, even though technically he was a looter, and therefore by the laws of the state liable to be shot where he stood.

'Shall I load them up?'

'Sure, I'll help you. Get the others in too; we'll put 'em in the cart under a tarp in case it rains. You can take charge of the cart.'

'Yep, I'll hitch up some horses from our stables, and we'll make sure that that we have enough bullets for the rifles. Will we take the cannon too?'

'If we can take it, but I don't know what the hell it's doing here.' By this time, Clay and Holt had arrived.

'I can tell you,' said Clay. 'Old Giles, he was in the army during the Civil War and he kept that cannon as something like a memento, but for a serious purpose too. It was a defence against anyone who might want to raid the village. Guess he didn't have time to wheel it out given the nature of the true raid.' The girl bowed her head and went outdoors. She followed Ryan as he went and fetched a low buckboard, hitching his horse to it and bringing it to the front of the building.

'Kegs of gunpowder?' The girl looked bemused by the whole thing.

'Yep. Well, you see, farmers and ranchers like to clear their land of trees,' said Ryan. 'Some of the manpower involved would be too much if they didn't have help to bring them down. I've used gunpowder a few times on the ranch.'

'This does not look like a mere scouting expedition,' said the girl as Hawk and his men came out with the kegs and began to load them on to the buckboard.

'I can answer that, Miss,' said Hawk. 'When you're going into a den full of snakes you want to take a sword with you. This is our sword.' They finished loading the kegs, while the cannon was the worst thing of all; it took three of them to get it aboard. The buckboard was now so heavy that the horse could barely pull it along.

'It's all right,' said Ryan, 'this is just for the moment. There'll be a team hitched to this particular wagon.' He led the horse to the edge of the woods where he unhitched it, then concealed the wagon by covering it in loose brushwood from their surroundings.

Yancey sat in the small jail. He felt the king of his domain because he was not in a cell while the other two were. It was a small cell capable of holding two men at a time, and that was as a holding area because there was only one bunk. Scott glared out at the huge man who had been so instrumental in their earlier plans.

'What do you think you're doing? You're just as much a prisoner here as the rest of us.'

'That fact may be the case,' said Yancey, 'but shut yore yaps or you'll get this.' He waved a meaty fist and laughed. The main door of the building opened and

111

Ryan appeared. There was a look on his face that said he was not looking forward to what he had to say, but it was a job that he had to do.

'You two, Yancey, I have something to ask of you.' He stepped into the building. 'I wanted to see all three of you hang for what you did to me and the girl. You still might: kidnapping is a mighty serious offence.'

'We were just getting what was my due,' snarled Scott.

'If you thought that, you sure went about it the wrong way. But I have a proposition for you guys, one that'll help you, me and the villagers.' He explained the proposal to them in a short, sharp way, then let his words hang in the air.

'That,' said Scott, 'sounds to me like the most stupid thing I ever heard in my life.'

'Bandits? They took Bert?' asked Yancey who seemed to have a particular affection for that individual. 'Bert, I'd like to look for him.'

'You'd be as well throwing yerself off that weir outside this village,' said Scott.

'What about you?' asked Ryan, looking straight at Jardine. 'Want to be left here to stew while we're out scouting, only to get yore neck stretched when we come back?'

The prisoner had a haunted look about him; clearly he was between the biggest of rocks and the worst of hard places. He looked to his companion for some sort of guidance.

'So are you going to give us transport?' asked Scott.

'I sure am,' answered Ryan promptly.

'Then we'll go,' said his cousin, 'long as we don't need

112

to fight nobody.'

'As I said, this is a scouting expedition,' said Ryan. 'We're sounding out the lay of the land. No one will get killed, I swear.'

'Then we'll go,' said Scott. 'I speak for Mack and Yancey too.'

'Good, I'll be back for you shortly,' said Ryan. 'Just a few more things to do.' He went out and locked the door.

'What the hell was that about?' asked Mack. 'From what I gathered this place was raided by a bunch of bandits. They – Hawk and the rest – might think they're going to sneak about, but the bandits might have other ideas.'

'You ain't thinking clear with that coconut you call a head,' said Scott. 'They're goin' to give us transport, that means horses, and there's plenty of thick branches lying around that can act as clubs.'

'They'll shoot us if we try to ride off.'

'That's right – at first, that is – so what we does is tag along until we're well away from all this, then we sneaks out.' All of these words had been exchanged between them in whispers because Scott was sneaking covert glances at the traitor, Yancey. Mack relaxed at the reassurances: there was a lot of country out there, Texas being the biggest state in the union. They could get away at their leisure long before they ever encountered any bandits, and when the others were distracted by their mission. Ryan came back about half an hour later.

'That's everything ready. No time like the present,' he said, 'so what's your answer, guys? The rope or an expedition to help other people?'

113

'I'll go,' said Yancey surging to his feet, inactivity not suiting him at all.

'We're in,' said Scott, with what he hoped looked like a genuine smile, but was more like the rictus grin of a man staring death in the face.

CHAPTER SIXTEEN

It was not hard to find the motivation of his men, thought Aguste Rivero. Most of them came from poor villages across the Mexican side of the Brazos River. Most of them knew about the way in which the land across from them had been annexed by the Americans in the days after the famous battle of the Alamo, a moment that had acted as a turning point in the formation of the Lone Star State. It had not been hard for him to stir their nationalism because most of the men he had recruited would have ended up as bandits, or as *vaqueros* working with the huge herds of cattle that fed both his own country and the hated USA.

He was walking past the fenced compound as he thought these things. It was late in the day and most of the prisoners were lying in their shelters or walking aimlessly around. One or two dared to look at him but they were swiftly ordered to stop doing so by barked orders from the guards.

Rivero firmly rejected the thought that his men were
bandits. The reason they had got this far was precisely
because they were not bandits; they were trained soldiers
and he had made sure that this was the case. He and
Ramirez had both been in the Mexican army – indeed
they had fought in many battles – and they had made
sure that they had retreated to Rivero's sprawling
hacienda in the north country and drilled the men into
their ways, rejecting any who were too wild or lacked dis-
cipline.

He had created a well-disciplined, hearty body of men
who were ready to follow him in his cause; in that he
could be happy. Some had baulked at the idea of capturing a village of the gringos, but such was the force of his
personality that he had persuaded them that he was not
mad, only idealistic. Of course the promise of gold and
silver had been the point that had swung them in his
favour. They were happy to take a huge risk for huge
rewards, and so was he. The thing was, the reward he was
looking for was quite different from theirs. He had not
told them this, but he hoped that the capture of the west-
erners would get a great deal of attention from the
leaders of the government and send shockwaves through
the southwest, and stir those who had their land annexed
without their permission to rebel. He was even prepared
to become a martyr to this cause and go down fighting
along with his men. He had not told any of them this
either, fearing that his readiness to throw away his own
life was not one in which they wanted to sacrifice theirs.

These thoughts were interrupted when Ramirez
appeared, grinning, with a number of their men, jan-

gling a set of keys in his hand.

'Ah, I see you have decided to entertain the men after all,' said Rivero. There was some distaste in his tone, but he knew this was part of what soldiers liked to do, part of their rights of conquest.

'Do not kill anyone and make sure they are fit for the hills,' he said. Ramirez opened the gates, and the prisoners looked up and saw the second-in-command and the men who were with them, and they reacted by moving away. Those who had been sleeping woke up, and they too moved away from the bandits. The men took two women each, picking the younger ones and herding them forward, while Ramirez picked another: Lena. The other women were older and more experienced, but she was young. Bert immediately realized what was happening and stood in front of the men as they pushed and prodded their captives towards the gate.

'No,' he said, 'no, this is wrong. Don't do this, for the sake of God; this is only a young girl. These are respectable women.' He got no further, sensing that his words would stir up trouble. Ramirez lifted his Winchester, used it as a club and hit the older man on the side of the head. Bert gave a loud groan and fell to the ground, and would not wake again for a long time.

As Ramirez pulled her past Rivero, Lena tore free from his grasp and knelt at the foot of the leader.

'Please, this is terrible, horrible. I have never been with a man.' Ramirez pulled her roughly to her feet, but Rivero looked at her with a strange expression on his face as Ramirez grabbed her. Ramirez started to lead her away, but he was halted by his commander.

'No,' said Rivero, 'this one is mine.'

'To the victor goes the spoils, eh?' said Ramirez, letting go of the girl and pushing her towards Rivero, his tone showing that he was more than a little displeased with this turn of events. The women were weeping as they were led off, and a whole group of the prisoners were up against the fence, knowing what was happening.

Calmly the guards moved the women along the length of the parade ground and into the buildings in which the so-called troops were billeted. In the meantime, Rivero led the young woman towards his own quarters, barely touching her, but with the air of someone who has won a trophy. The yelling, protesting prisoners gradually fell silent and returned to their meagre shelters as the cold air came in and the night descended.

'You and your ideas,' snarled Mack at the person who had once been his friend. 'Get horses, you said, ride off, you said. Look at us now.' Scott McArthur remained silent but with a look of chagrin on his face as he handled the reins of one of the horses in front of him. There was a long-suffering look on his face. Behind them rode Abbey, bearing a gun at her side. Hawk was not one to waste resources and the young woman was as fit, or fitter, than any of the men. She was dressed in canvas trousers, a waistcoat and checked shirt, and her blonde hair was hidden beneath a wide-brimmed cowboy hat of soft felt.

Only the two young men, her former captors, were not riding horses. Instead they were driving the buckboard along the uneven trail that had been created along the banks of the Brazos by the hundreds and thousands of cattle that came along here every year during the cattle drives. Neither were they unaware of the contents of the flat, utilitarian transport, and winced every time they went over a bump or when one of the wheels descended into one of the many depressions in the ground to be found on the makeshift road.

At first, when she learned that the two men who had taken her from her home were going with them, Abbey had wanted to shoot them as soon as they were taken from the jail, but when Hawk had explained their role in the expedition, Abbey had agreed, knowing with almost sadistic glee that this would be worse torture than anything her mind could devise.

Beside her rode Yancey on a horse that looked like a pony due to his enormous size. They had been relegated to the back of the party, and Hawk had privately asked her to keep an eye on Yancey in case he showed any signs of wanting to help his fellow kidnappers.

Beside her – and barely saying a word – was Ryan, who had an expression on his face that showed he was not too pleased at having to play nursemaid to a young woman and his bad-hearted cousin. In fact he had argued back in Hatton Falls that they should not be exposing the young woman to any danger and that she should be left behind. Hawk had pointed out that if they left her she would be alone until Lamington and the other ranchers returned. But at least he had got his father to agree that whatever happened on this expedition, the young woman would not be at the heart of the action. They had started late in the day, which meant that they had not yet

119

caught up with the bandits who had robbed an entire village of its population.

It wasn't long before they struck camp, but not down by the open riverbank: Hawk was cautious enough to draw them back into the thick woodlands that bordered the mighty river.

'I can see a natural rock formation down by the water,' he said, 'under which they would have sheltered. They have left many signs of their passing, such as hoof prints from their horses, but this is the biggest sign of all: fires have been made here, bones thrown away and skins and feathers left from their prey, and there are even signs that the people must have slept here.'

'But it's cold at night,' protested Ryan.

'I don't think they would have worried about a few casualties,' said Hawk grimly, 'do you?'

They set up several A-frame tents and made sure that there was a guard roster for the tent inhabited by McArthur and Jardine. Ryan, who was not feeling the slightest bit sleepy and who was still full of anger, was the first on duty. Hawk, despite being the oldest of the group, would take over from him in the early hours and grab some more shuteye before they left. Ryan made sure that Scott and Mack saw him finger his Colt .45 in a loving fashion as they made their way to their bedrolls.

'Just give me one chance,' he said thoughtfully, 'one chance.' The intense look on his thin features and his low, thoughtful tone did more to instil terror in his captives than any amount of ranting and raving.

Being used to cattle drives and having to make camp, the three cowboys were not the least bit troubled by their circumstances – in fact the tents were a luxury for them as sometimes they spent weeks in their bedrolls under the stars.

Ryan went on duty, and it was a long grim watch in the darkness of the woods. Hawk had estimated that they were still reasonably far from the enemy, so they had lit a fire, but made sure the smoke was dispersed amongst the thick canopy above, and they had used good dry wood that gave off a lot less smoke in the first place. Now he only had the dying embers and his thoughts for company as he sat there wrapped in a horse-blanket, facing the tent of the enemy within, gun ready at his side. However, the noises from within the tent indicated that his former partners were sleeping soundly, apparently without a troubled conscience between them.

There was a rustle of undergrowth and he was immediately alert, but a slim, female form put a finger on his lips.

'Any room under that blanket?' asked Abbey, and his reply was to let her under and snuggle into his side, suddenly aware that his heart was beating a great deal faster than before. He was just grateful for her warmth and the company, he said internally, but his body reacted to her feminine presence in a way that told a different story. He was aroused by her, and something told him she knew this and didn't mind. The long night wore on.

CHAPTER
SEVENTEEN

Next morning everyone was still yawning and feeling tired, particularly the captives who, despite having slept better than anyone, seemed to be stumbling about in a daze. Hawk suspected that they were not used to a regular lifestyle and usually kept in bed until noon before wasting their worthless lives stealing, then drinking and gambling in the nearest saloon. Once the horses were fed – and they came first – the party took in a good breakfast of freshly caught game roasted over the newly revived fire. Once this was done they made sure the fire was extinguished by piling earth on top and stamping it down and using water from their canteens – which they refilled in the river – saddled up the horses and got going.

Scott was not about to let them away with their aims. 'What in the name of the Brazos do you think old Hawk is up to? He sure ain't bringing along all this hardware so he can hold a picnic with them bandits. Yore all set to get yourselves killed – and us with you.'

'So?' said Holt. 'You want to keep stirring it,

McArthur, we'll silence your peep. And I'll tell you some-thing else: you betray us to them savage invaders, I'll shoot you personally.'

'Just saying,' said Scott, but he became uncommonly pale and silent. Jardine, riding on the buckboard beside him, just looked as if he would be elsewhere. In fact he looked as if he was going though hell, a fact that pleased Ryan, who was still riding shotgun on the two along with girl.

A few hours later Hawk held up his hand and halted the entire party with a low command. He was looking at the trail in front of them. 'There's been a lot going on here.' He got off his horse, signalling his riders to follow, and went into the woodlands, his eyes picking up signs that none of the others could even see. That was when they came across the three shallow graves.

Because they had not been buried for long, woodland animals had not yet made inroads into the bodies. With the help of his son, Hawk uncovered the faces of the dead people, two men and one woman.

'George Ransome, Tilly Voe, Dag Meershel,' he recited in a calm but somehow deadly tone. Somehow, finding the bodies was a turning point in what had hap-pened. Up until then their mission had seemed more about the trip and less about what they would find at the end of the road, wherever that happened to be. Abbey stood beside the bodies and hot tears fell from her eyes, but they were tears of anger.

'It is time,' said Hawk, turning to look at the group who had followed him all this way, putting their faith in him.

123

'Time for what?' asked McArthur, looking genuinely bewildered, and even a little scared, although this was something to which he would never admit.

'There is an old tribal saying,' said Hawk. 'A man of stealth can do much hunting and kill more enemies than a man who rushes into battle. We are not going to win anything by going in there openly. When I spoke to old Betsy she told me there must have been at least fifty of them, all with horses and all armed. Now that is a small army in these parts, and they must have either taken the prisoners across the river and into Mexico or they have them holed up somewhere.'

'You mean to a peasant village?' asked Ryan.

'Or something much bigger; we know the cattle trail goes past an old government building set into the hills, so that's where we must go.'

'To the camp?'

'No, to the hills.'

With regret, Hawk abandoned the buckboard, but not just by leaving it where it could be found by a casual passer-by – not that many of those were to be found around here – so he had it concealed deep in the woodland, and then he had the kegs of gunpowder loaded into panniers. The cannon was more of a problem but he made a travois with the help of his son, which was a kind of makeshift sled constructed out of fallen branches, and this was attached to ropes and towed behind a horse.

Mack and McArthur were given the horses that had pulled the buckboard, and were warned that because of where they were there was a real chance that if they rode

124

off on their own they risked running into bandit patrols.

'Besides,' Clay told them, 'you run I'll blow off yore darned heads.'

Hawk was not just randomly taking them away from the cattle trail. He had lived in this county most of his life, he had farmed here, he had explored and he had hunted game in these hills with his father when times were hard, and he had the uncanny ability to memorise locations the way others remembered faces. Soon he discovered a pass that no one else would have known about unless they had an intimate knowledge of the district.

'This is called Savage Wolf Pass,' he said. 'It's where, one winter, some travellers were eaten by wolves. That was a terrible winter, I remember it well, and we lost a lot of cattle that year.'

The pass was so narrow that only two horses could be led through at a time. Holt and Clay took up the rear while Hawk and Ryan led at the front. It was immediately clear that they were on an upward climb and the path on which they walked was uneven and littered with stones. Once or twice, not only the men but also the horses stumbled, and given that they were carrying gunpowder in their panniers this was not good news.

Finally, after what seemed like hours, although it was barely more than one, the pass widened out and they found that they were once more in a wooded area replete with ponderosa pines, silver birches and oak trees. They all seemed to breathe a little more easily but they were all aching and breathless because it had been a fairly steep climb.

'What the hell was the point of that?' said Scott, losing

all caution.

'I'll show you, I'll show all of you,' answered Hawk, 'just keep your heads low and back off immediately.'

To their left was a stony ridge. He led them towards this and crouched down as he reached the side, signalling for them to do the same. They all obeyed, knowing instinctively that this was a situation in which none of the party wanted to be seen. Finding the bodies had been a grim warning that they were not on some Sunday outing, but now they were faced with stark reality.

There, set back from the hills, with grey walls and manned guard towers, was Camp Brazos, the old prisoner of war building from the Civil War. They were almost level with the guard towers on that side of the building, and as Hawk pulled back so did the rest. They were so close that a loud shout from one of them could have been heard on the other side.

They were in real, deadly danger, and their lives would depend on their actions over the next few hours.

Hawk brought an object out from his breast pocket. It was a retractable spyglass, a good one, the top and bottom bound with brass. 'Used to use this all the time when I was out with Pa,' he said. 'Helped keep an eye on the cattle. Some of them mavericks roamed far and wide.' The rest had retreated now, but he made his way back to the bluff, lay on his stomach and surveyed the prison.

He came back and looked at his companions. 'They've opened the gates and it looks like they're herding the villagers out.'

'You mean taking them away again?' asked Flynn, with

a faint tone of asperity in his voice. 'More trailing for us.'

'No, I don't mean that at all,' said Hawk, 'they're armed with shovels and picks – looks to me as if they're heading somewhere.' He waited for a while longer, with the rest of the riders looking on and waiting for what he had to say. He closed the eyeglass and pulled away from the bluff. His voice was low as he came back to the group and stood with them. 'Time to go, I think,' he said. 'They're heading straight for us.'

This was not good news for a group of people who were exhausted, who had just arrived at the very spot where they thought they were going to be able to rest, but the guards pushing the villagers up the steep hill that led to where they were hiding were heavily armed, and would not hesitate to murder them on the spot. They could fight back, but they all knew that the attackers would have the advantage.

Attack was also the best form of defence, but Hawk did not want to do this either since it would give their presence away far too early.

He took the lead and led his horse through the pines and along the undulating landscape, once more finding a pass that led between two steep hills, looking back now and then to make sure the others were following. Once or twice Scott and Mack stumbled and there was a thud or two that made him frown, and the horses whickered a few times at protest in having to continue. He could only hope that the sounds of the prisoners, the shouting of the guards and the rising incline of the bluff from which they were retreating would hide the sounds from their would-be attackers. He was also worried about Yancey,

127

who was making growls that sounded like the rumble of distant thunder. Yancey could very well go berserk and lead a one-man attack of his own, but luckily the big man was wedged between those at the back and Hawk in the lead, and seemed inclined to keep following the leader.

At last the area opened up and they found they were in a sort of bowl between the hills, where the lush spring grass grew freely and there was a bit more heat in the air. More importantly, the sounds of the climbing people had vanished into the distance. This did not mean that they could not be found if they made too much noise and armed bandits appeared ready to shoot.

'What the hell are they up to?' asked Clay. 'They got the prisoners, restored the prison, now they're digging in the hills? It don't make sense.'

'The White Mines,' said Hawk, with a thoughtful expression on his face. Naturally he and the others were mindful enough to talk in low voices.

'What are you talking about?' asked Scott, with a guarded expression. Flynn shoved him in the back and the girl glared at him.

'Rumours abound in these places,' said Hawk. 'The Civil War sure shook up everything around here. For years there was chaos and I remember the old camp when the last troops left – I was a boy at the time. But there was a time long before this, told in the legends of my people.'

'Legends,' snorted Flynn who was a practical kind of man.

'Many stories have a basis in fact,' said Hawk. 'Indians have a way of looking after their world. If they dig in the

earth for a mineral of any kind, they believe that something has to be returned to the earth, and it was said that
the Cherokee around here had gold artefacts – ceremo-
nial arrowheads, headdress decorations and the like –
and it was thought they had traded the gold with other
tribes from the south.'

'That wasn't the case?' asked Ryan.

'No, the true story that the new rulers never got to
know was that the Cherokee in these lands had found a
rich seam of gold inside the hills. One seam, but big
enough for their purposes, but you see the Indians look
on gold as being less precious than water or meat. It is
not essential for survival,' said Hawk. 'They took enough
for decoration, and went back from time to time for that
which they needed.'

'Seems you knew enough about it,' said Flynn.

'It was a story, passed down through the tribes,' said
Hawk, 'like the story of how the moon was formed or why
the sun god shines. They were called the White Mines
because they were in the hills that shone so white in the
rising sun.'

'If this is true, why has it not come out before?'

'The truth is, it did. But you must understand, even
from my early years, this part of the US has been in
turmoil. This land was once Mexican, and was taken over
as part of the treaty of Guadalupe Hidalgo. A lot of
Mexican overlords would have wanted to get to the
mines – they talked to the Indians a great deal more than
the white man – but these lands are sacred to my brother
ancestors and they would have had to fight the local
tribes. That is not a problem they face today.' He made

the last remark without a trace of bitterness, but the men present knew exactly what he meant – or at least the other riders did. Along with the other Indian tribes, the Cherokee had been relocated to reservations even though it was rumoured that pockets of them could still be found roaming about these very hills. So it was unlikely that there would be anyone to defend their ancestral spots. It also explained why some of their old overlords had returned to exploit a place that was far from legend to them. A rich seam of gold that did not yield mere fragments could be worth millions.

They all fell silent, knowing that in the bowels of the earth around them the villagers were digging to save their lives.

CHAPTER EIGHTEEN

The night was the thing. The guards in the towers might have been watchful, but it was mostly towards the prisoners who might try to escape, and later on only the towers that overlooked the front of the prison were manned. In theory that should have given enough warning, but the towers at the back of the prison had hills behind them, and since it was spring the lush vegetation that grew in this area had sprang up beside the very walls of the building. It would have taken the work of many men to clear the area, and what immediately became clear to Hawk was that the invaders – whoever they were – did not have a huge amount of manpower.

It was obvious that they were not going to retreat from where they were, but Ryan was wounded by the words of his father.

'Rye, I want you to go back to Hatton Falls and tell what you have seen here. You have to let them know what's going on; give them the layout of the prison and the numbers we have observed of the invaders, and take the girl with you.'

'I won't do it, I want to be here, and God knows what they've done to Lena and the rest.'

'I know what you are saying, but your mission is the most important one of all. We're fighting against those who have taken what is ours. They are ruthless killers and they will work those villagers to death in pursuit of what they want.'

'I want to stay too,' protested Abbey. 'Those poor people . . . I don't know what it's like underground, but I know it will be hot, dusty, thirsty work. We have to help them.'

'And what would it be like if they captured us?' asked Hawk. 'What would they do to a fine young lady like you?' He spoke slowly and deliberately, looking into her face as he did so because he wanted to scare her. She blanched and pulled away from him.

'No, I can't have that,' her hand fluttered to her face in distress. 'I've already had what men can do to me.' Ryan looked at her distress and knew that he could not be a party to making it worse.

'All right, I'll go, and I'll take Abbey too, but once she's safe and there's a warning out, I'm coming back.'

'In the meantime we'll make a plan for action,' promised Hawk, 'and there will be an attack on these bandits. They can't get away with this. If they do, they'll come back and it will be even worse, I know their type.'

By this time it was late in the afternoon, and as with all things there was no time like the present. Ryan and Abbey were kitted out with all that they would need to take them back to the village, and Hawk instructed his son to stay back from the trail and in the woodlands when they camped overnight. With two horses and barely anything to carry they would be back at the village before the middle of the day, and when they told their story to whatever posse had gathered, Ryan at least would be able to return with them long before the end of the next day. With that promise in mind, along with knowing that he was helping to defeat a dangerous enemy, Ryan made his way out of the encampment with Abbey. He looked back once as they went through the pass on the far side, leading their horses, and Hawk was standing looking at them. He saw Ryan and nodded once. Ryan nodded in return.

As they descended to the woodlands below, they entered the most dangerous part of their mission, for they might alert those who had kidnapped an entire village. But it was the first day of working the mines and the militants had only a limited amount of manpower, which meant that they would be distracted by so much work for so few people.

They were down on the edge of the woodland trail within about half an hour. The descent had not been without its problems, since they had often encountered steep stretches where the horses might have gone too fast and injured their legs.

They were on the main trail with their steeds when there was a noise in front of them and a party of the bandits appeared. They were big men, and from the poles strung with antelope and rabbits that hung from their shoulders, it was obvious that they had been out hunting to supply the needs of the prison camp. If Ryan had been on his own he would have dug his spurs into the side of his horse and charged off, risking their shots, but the girl had frozen to the spot and she was not even on her horse. The group consisted of five bandits, and one of them, who was clearly the leader, was armed with a Winchester '73 that he was pointing at the girl's head.

'Gringos,' he said, 'surrender and all will be well for you. Otherwise you die.' Regretfully, Ryan got off his horse. He and his father had forgotten one salient fact: there would always be a hunting party in the forest because feeding so many people until all the gold had been located and mined would be a top priority. Even the prisoners would not be starved because they would be needed for their labour. By this time the other members of the hunting party had dropped the prey they had been gathering and had withdrawn fearsome looking handguns from their belts. The girl was still speechless now that their worst nightmare had come true.

'We have it with her,' said one of the bandits, looking at the girl's young taut breasts as they strained against the fabric of her shirt.

'No,' said their leader, 'Ramirez has first choice, you know that, and we need to get this food back.' Their hands were tied and they were led off into ignominy.

Up on the hill, spying on the prison with his eyeglass, Hawk saw his son and the girl being led into captivity and with a gut-wrenching certainty knew that by trying to make them safe he had put them on the greatest danger of all.

'I'm going down there,' said Hawk, 'and if family means

anything to you, Scott, you're coming with me.' It was later at night and it was getting towards darkness. Scott looked at the man who suddenly seemed to have gone mad, and for the first time he seemed to have a clear mind towards what was happening.

'If you go down there and try to fire your way into an armed fort, you'll die, and what's more they'll know there's more of us and they'll hunt us down and kill us too.' Hawk stared at the young man, who had made a reasonable point. Hawk had a wild expression and looked more like one of his ancestors on his father's side than ever, his Indian blood rising as he thought of the capture of his only surviving son.

'No, that is not what I mean, and if you and Mack want to survive the rope you'll do what I ask of you.' Then he made his request.

Their task would have been almost impossible if it had not been for the shape of the Pinto hills, but the fort was set in an undulating landscape and it allowed the three men to do what they had set out to do, which was to distribute the kegs of gunpowder at different points in the building. To prevent a foot patrol from finding them with just a cursory look, Hawk had them covered with green leaves and set in close to the walls and had the other two do the same.

He had Yancey carry a load of the kegs in a backpack, but did not allow the big man to come further along than the bottom of the hill. There was no one in the towers at the back, but even so Yancey was needed for his strength, not his ability to display stealth. With this in mind, the three men took four kegs each off him and moved along the side and back of the fort implanting them. The whole process took barely half an hour but it was a nerve-racking time for all three. However, Hawk knew that the young men were good at stealth, and they had the sharp eyes and the speed of youth. For all that, the three of them knew that if one guard spotted them the shooting would begin. They were helped, though, by the noise within the fort itself, because the bandits were celebrating their discovery of the white mines and their leader – whoever he was – was letting them do so in his own interests.

They assembled back at the foothills behind the fort, not even daring to breathe more easily as Hawk led them away into the darkness. Without their leader the other three men would have stumbled around in what would have been an increasingly desperate situation. But Hawk had set down some hot embers in a spot further away from the fort. These were in a food tin that still glowed a faint cherry red. He used these to light some dry grass and lit a torch he had left in the same spot. With this he was able to lead them to another spot in the back of the hills where they were able to start climbing towards their camp.

If the flame of their torch was seen they would be fired upon immediately, and the four of them felt as if they were hardly daring to breathe, but they kept climbing and at last they found they were back at their camp overlooking the prison where a low fire flickered between the trees.

'I hope that was worth it,' said Scott. 'What if your plan doesn't work?'

'I'm exhausted,' said Mack as he went to his tent and crawled inside.

'You shoulda let me fight,' growled Yancey.

'To answer you all in order,' said Hawk, 'Scott, if it doesn't work, it doesn't work. Mack is right, we all have to sleep, and as for you, Yancey, if things go the way I think they will you'll get your chance to fight.'

'How?' asked Scott. 'There's a lot more of them than there is of us.' He was direct enough to ask a question that was on all of their minds, because the three riders, Holt, Flynn and Clay all had the same questioning manner.

'There is a saying from my father's tribe,' said Hawk, 'stealth is wealth. We have done the first part of our task, and now we need more stealth to complete what has to be done – and we all have Winchester rifles and plenty of ammunition.' The look on his face was such that no one continued questioning him.

'They took that girl,' said Flynn, and the look on his face said all they needed to know about what he would do if they harmed her.

'Let us sleep,' said Hawk. 'They won't harm anybody right now because they've go a limited time to get the gold, and they know it, but they'll be up at dawn to continue – only we'll be up much earlier.' They went away to their respective tents and tried to sleep, his expression staying with them as much as his final words.

CHAPTER NINETEEN

Hawk knew something about his men that he had never really discussed with them. They were all great shots with rifles, though not so much with handguns. There was a simple reason for this: in the early days the ranch was apt to being attacked by bandits and hostile Indians, and so were those who worked there. Every single one of the riders had at some point had to lead an attack against another man, or even, working together, a group of men.

When they had come with him on this so-called 'scouting' mission, every single one of them had known that this might end in some kind of confrontation. Indeed, if the villagers had been abducted by some band of roaming thugs, there was a good chance that these would have been detected, attacked, and the villagers freed by now. Hawk, too, was no mean exponent of the rifle, and despite his heritage he had defended his own vigorously in the past. As far as he was concerned this was just more of the same.

'This is what we're going to do,' he said when they were awake in the early hours just before dawn. They were all gathered together, eating some cold food and drinking from their canteens. 'We're all going to up our positions. You, Logan, are going to get to the far side of the fort. You'll take up position at the back, Alonzo.' Clay nodded at this, although he looked a trifle disappointed not to be at the main action. 'Frank, you and I will do what has to be done from the bluff on either side of the mine. That's going to be the most dangerous part. Are you up for it?'

'Sure am,' said Flynn with an expression on his face that showed he was ready for anything after what he had seen. They had all witnessed the weary, half-starved villagers being led away from the mine after toiling there all day and early evening in hellish conditions. Some had already died getting to the prison, but a lot more would be dead from their backbreaking labour before the gold was all mined – and they had heard the whoops of joy from the bandits when it was discovered.

Yancey sat with them, and Hawk turned and looked at the big man. 'You made a mistake when you got involved with those two fools,' he said. 'Are you prepared to help defend everything that is ours?'

'Hoha, a giving of mines to you it should be,' said Yancey, breathing heavily through his broad nose like a bull. 'Charge them, kill and kill, that's what it should be.'

Everyone looked a little askance at this; Yancey was the loosest of loose cannons. Speaking of which, Hawk had already had this set up in a strategic position. It was the turn of the two former kidnappers now. They were yawning and looked half-dead, being more used to going to bed at this hour than getting up.

'I'm going to arm you with guns,' said Hawk grimly. 'You'll do as I ask, and if you don't – if you run or turn on us – we'll show you no mercy, for you won't just be kidnappers anymore, you'll be traitors.' The two young men nodded vigorously and would have protested that they were not that bad, but Hawk gave them a withering look and they sank into sleepy silence.

Not one of those present doubted the boldness of what they were about to do, but none were going to back out now. They began to take up their positions. The signal for action would be one loud rifle shot in the air from Hawk, while the result from then onwards would be in the lap of the gods.

As Mack and Scott made their way down towards the tree line that faced the side of the mine, Scott seemed more quiet and brooding than normal.

'What is it?' asked Mack. 'We can do this – don't shoot anybody, I mean – just get out of here, into the wood-lands and away.'

'He's right, though,' said Scott suddenly, 'we would be guilty of treason against our own country: think about it. 'Sides, I've just thought of something you haven't . . . but you was never that good at working things out. They've got gold, not just traces, but actual mined nuggets. We'll deal with Hawk later – but some or most of that gold is gonna be ours.'

Self-interest was a powerful thing, and Mack bright-ened at the prospect of easy riches. 'An' we don't even go out there then? We wait until the dust has settled and then go in?'

Scott did not even deign to answer this, and the interminable wait continued as they looked from the tree towards the gaping hole of the White Mine set below the bluff above which Hawk and his men waited.

At last the gates of the fort were opened and the villagers were led out, equipped with their picks and shovels and led by a group of about ten armed men who had fearsome-looking bullet belts across their chests. The guards carried various kinds of rifle, including the very type that was going to be used against them. Some of the prisoners carried backpacks, probably containing enough food and water to last them for the day. It was a pitiful sight, because the villagers were still wearing the clothes in which they had been abducted, and these were wearing badly and were dusty, torn and sweat-stained. The guards and the villagers toiled up the hill that led towards the entrance of the mine. The villagers were forced inside first, some of them carrying the oil lamps that were their only means of illumination in the hell inside.

Ten guards did not seem a lot from the garrison, but some of the bandits were out gathering food in the forest, some were sleeping and others had been assigned to guard the prison, while yet more were cooking food, looking after the horses, and preparing for the prisoner's return.

The only two prisoners who looked fairly well were Scott and Abbey. They walked side by side and they both had bruises on their faces and probably on other places that could not be seen. It was obvious that there had been some sort of altercation involving the pair of them after they had been taken prisoner. Scott felt his heart

141

leap in his chest at the sight of his cousin: when the shooting began he would have his chance to fell someone he had been brought up to hate, someone who had been handed the privileges his poor cousin had never been able to enjoy. One stray bullet, that was all it would take, and no one would ever know the act was deliberate.

His train of thought was interrupted when there was a noise that broke the air that had only previously echoed to the marching footsteps of the prisoners and their guards: it was the sound of a rifle being fired up in the air.

Now that the sound had rung out, it might have been expected that whoever was attacking would fire at the guards. This was not the case, for it had been a signal for a series of shots to crack through the air of the hills towards Camp Brazos. The first two targets taken out were the guards in the tower – they had been handled from either side, with one of the guards screaming as he staggered backwards, a hole in his chest as he plummeted to the ground, but he was dead before he landed.

The other shots from the concealed men, triggered by the one Hawk had fired from the bluff, were aimed at the barrels of gunpowder that were concealed at the side of the building. Rivero had not inaugurated a foot patrol for the simple reason that he needed his men for either hunting or shepherding the prisoners, and luckily for Hawk and his companions the concealment had worked. There was a rumbling sound as each barrel was hit by the superb marksmanship of the riders, and the gunpowder, rich in chemicals, reacted to the glowing heat from the bullets by giving forth an explosion out of all proportions to the size of the kegs used. There was a kind of chain reaction, too, with one explosion interacting with another so that there was a wall of fire on either side of the building. The walls were made of brick and adobe like many of the buildings in the area, and might have been able to withstand one hit, but since these were all together they combined into a force that was too much to withstand. As in the battle of Jericho, the walls came crumbling down.

Up on the bluff, Hawk dared to look over and saw the blossoming flames and the falling stones, but there was no time to dwell on the way his plans had come to fruition. The guards with the prisoners had heard him firing the signal and they ran forwards to the source of the sound, rifles at the ready.

The entrance to the mines was just below where they had first made camp, but the hills were not especially steep and it was possible for men who were fit enough to run up the slope to the side of the mine entrance and reach the area above, which is what the guards were doing.

Ryan and the rest of the prisoners shuffled towards the mines, because their ankles were bound with ropes that allowed them to walk, but with hardly any play for more than one stride at a time. This meant nobody was able to run off, and if they tried to untie their bonds they would get a blow from one of their captors. Now that the guards were distracted, Ryan bent down and quickly freed the ropes from around his legs and those of Abbey.

143

'Run for the trees,' he told her.

'No, I'm coming with you,' she said. He did not argue with her but ran after the troops who were set on capturing the bluff. He did not know what they would be able to do, but he was going to stand with his father.

But Hawk had seen what was happening and a handgun came spinning through the air and landed at Ryan's feet. He picked it up, but he fumbled with the Colt. As he did so one of the guards turned and saw that a former prisoner was armed and aimed his rifle straight at Ryan's head, while the latter was still fumbling to hold the gun properly, and a little off-balance. It was obvious that Ryan was going to be shot in the head before he could even aim at his enemy.

The guard was a big Mexican with impressive facial hair who had nothing but contempt for the gringos who had stolen his heritage; he brought his weapon to bear and was actually squeezing his finger on the trigger when a shot rang out from the trees to the side of the bluff.

The Mexican gave a grunt like a man who has been thumped on the back and dropped the rifle. He put his hand to his side and felt the wetness where the bullet had entered, looked surprised, and dropped dead as his heart gave way.

Two men about the same age as Ryan ran from the trees as the remaining guards, hearing the shots, realized that they were under fire. Instead of continuing with their forward charge they began to run back down the slopes. But there was a melee as the villagers, seeing what was happening, began to panic, with many trying to run without loosing their bonds and falling down. Two of the guards fell over the prone villagers and were immediately attacked by the others before they could bring their rifles to bear. Another two were brought down by shots from the bluff, because Hawk was standing there like an avenging angel, a set look on his narrow features as he concentrated on killing his enemy while sparing his friends from the village. Two more of the men fell, while one of the remaining guards turned and fired at the man who was destroying their dreams. Hawk gave a groan and vanished from sight, because as is often the case, a lucky shot caught him before he could retreat.

Ryan gave a roar of rage and horror, and surged forward, hefted his gun . . . and this time he did not miss. His bullet took the man who had shot his father just as the so-called soldier turned to face him. The man fell, leaving behind only two men, who saw the way the tide was going and decided to run for the trees, performing the exact opposite action of Scott and Mack who had emerged from the same place. More shots rang out and the two men were felled, dropping their weapons and lying there groaning. Scott ran towards them and kicked the weapons away. He aimed his gun at the back of their heads as they lay there, one wounded in the shoulder and the other in the back.

'No,' shouted Abbey, coming forward and hastily picking up one of the rifles that lay beside the moaning soldiers. 'Don't do it, don't kill them, they can't hurt you anymore! But I can.' She lifted her rifle and aimed straight at his face. White-faced, Scott blanched at what he saw as his fate, and then he stood very still, a lack of movement that saved his life.

'I'm sorry,' he said, 'I was stupid, too stupid to see what I was doing.'

'Come on,' yelled Mack, 'don't you see? They're coming.' The others looked down the hills. The remaining troopers were spilling out of the ruined prison. Abbey saw that it was no time to settle personal scores, and she saw that the villagers were still milling around.

'All of you,' she yelled, 'come with me. Get up here to the side of the mine. Don't try to hide in the trees; they'll get among them and hunt you down.' People who had been bewildered and lost did what people do in such circumstances: they followed her up the slope and over the bluff that overhung the very mine in which they had toiled hard for so many hours. Her leadership had not come too soon for any of them because bullets were already flying in their direction and one of the villagers was struck. It was Bert, and he was wounded in the side, but with the help of Aimee and others he managed to stumble up and away from the oncoming troops.

Ryan was already over beside his father. Hawk was wounded, too, and the bullet had taken him in the shoulder. His face was an ashen grey with the pain, with a spreading blossom of red on his tunic as he tried to get to his feet. Ryan ignored what was happening around him as the villagers came over the rising bluff, urged on by Abbey, Scott and Mack. Ryan, with all the strength of his young body, got Hawk to his feet and half-supporting, half-carrying his father, got Hawk to walk away from the open area and back down to where the horses sheltered in amongst the trees.

'What's happening?' asked Hawk as his son grabbed a

146

horse blanket and helped him sit against a tree. Ryan ripped off part of his own shirt and bound the wound tightly. He knew the bullet was probably still in there, but luckily it seemed to have been deflected and had been the result of a ricochet rather than a direct hit, or it would have been much worse at that range. Ryan looked up at the slope that led to the very bluff where the villagers were now pouring in.

'They've had the sense to take the gun belts and weapons off the guards,' he said, 'now they're preparing to defend this area from Rivero ... Aguste Rivero, the man who financed all this. From the sound of it, I don't think they have much time.'

'Rivero? Good,' said Hawk, 'I can die happy thinking we struck back; we'll all die free men, not their prisoners.'

'You're not going to die,' said Ryan, 'but they are.' He spoke with a grim certainty he did not feel.

CHAPTER TWENTY

Rivero was in his private chambers when the attack happened. He was with the young girl, Lena, whom he had noticed just the previous day. He had spent the day in delicious anticipation of what he was going to do with the girl, but he was also extremely tired because he had spent days capturing, planning, working, supervising and berating the villagers. He was not just tired, he was exhausted and he had only just held his poise for his men. Besides, the girl had not been in the best of conditions, dusty and dishevelled with her hair a little matted. He had had her taken away to be cleaned up and given something suitable to wear, culled from whatever garments had been brought with them. With the walls finished and the first day of mining completed, he was finally able to do what he wanted and rest. The girl had slept in an antechamber where she had been given blankets and pillows while he had slept in the one proper bed provided within the prison, sinking deep in his own luxury, sleeping like one who was dead. The girl could have come through and smothered him in his sleep if she had known, but she had lain awake most of the time, her face white with fear.

Rested, in charge, with his men bringing him enough gold to finance the biggest of revolutions, Rivero set out to enjoy one of the fruits of his labour: the body of the girl.

He went through to her, the look on his face both patriarchal and lustful at the same time. He was calm and ready for this, the gift of what she had to offer. He had waited a long time for this, but he was a patient man – indeed he had waited years to carry out this conquest of his stolen lands, and better he did this when his body was relaxed and lustful rather than taken as some hasty meal that was consumed when tired and soon forgotten.

The girl was in her own room that had once obviously been an ante-room where the governor of the prison camp would have prepared for the day ahead, and a mirror on the wall had somehow survived the ravages of the years, showing him in his fine robe as he leaned over the straw bed on which the girl was lying. He woke her with a gentle shake. She sat up, knowing that the time had come, that the thing with which she had been going through torture in her own mind was about to happen.

'Do as I ask,' he said, 'and all will go well. It is a little thing, a symbol, and you will flower into womanhood.' She gasped and pulled away from him, trembling and he pulled her to her feet with strong hands. 'Am I that bad looking? I promise, if you are compliant and a willing companion, I will give you much of that desire. You are young, pretty . . . you can be at my side. I do not hate all gringos like some of my men; this has all been for a

149

purpose.' She allowed him to lead her into his bed-chamber. She seemed resigned to her fate, and was not even weeping or begging anymore for him to leave her alone, which was a pity in a way because such begging would only have increased his lust.

But even as he threw her onto the bed, the fort was racked by a series of explosions that made the chamber shake and heave as if there were a major earthquake going on. The girl was on her back on the bed now.

'Wait here,' he grated, hastily throwing off the robe and donning his trousers and jacket before running towards the doors of the bedchamber, throwing them wide and running downstairs. Once he was out in the courtyard, the scene that met his eyes was one of utter devastation. He was just in time to see the walls that he had made the people build crumble away like dust in the wind, while one of the towers was leaning to one side like a drunk after a party. His remaining men, some twenty-odd of them, were milling about the square in total disarray, but Ramirez came striding out to join his leader. He, too, had been hoping for some time off while the mines were being plundered – this, of course, had not happened.

'What is it?' he asked his leader. 'Is it the army?'

Rivero had quickly taken stock of the situation. He had noted that no troops were rushing in after the explosions, and he was a man who knew military tactics – he knew that such troops would have moved in immediately to secure the boundaries of the action.

'It's not the army, that is obvious,' he said. 'Rally the men and get them armed. We go out and face whoever is doing this.'

Ramirez did not waste any time because, like his leader, he knew that attack was the best form of defence. It was not long before the men were armed and ready to go out of the broken walls, with their two leaders in front, both armed with handguns in their waistbands and rifles in their hands.

It was Ramirez who had noticed that shooting was occurring on the side nearest the mine, and as his troops emerged he caught sight of the last villagers vanishing over the slope that led to the outputting rock formations above the mine. It did not take great intellect to surmise that someone had arranged the rescue of the villagers; their retreating forms and the dead bodies of his men attested only too starkly to this fact.

His men did not have to be told, but ran up the slope firing at will with Rivero in the lead. Ramirez, though, did something that on the face of it seemed surprising. He took three of his men and he turned to the land around the fort. There was a reason for this: Ramirez had been on the ground floor and he had heard the shots being fired that had set off the explosions. He knew that others were hiding in the hills. And this was shown to be true, because moment later a series of shots rang out that brought down some of the men who were running to catch the villagers.

Ramirez ducked behind the ruins with his men, using the jumbled rocks at the foot of the Pinto hills as a shelter for what he had to do. He and his three men waited until they saw the heads of the snipers appearing and shot directly at them. Clay, Holt and Flynn were pinned down; without seeing what they were aiming at they were now worse than useless, and it seemed from the withering fire they were under now that they had been detected and that it would prevent them from helping their companions.

In the meantime, Rivero was a spitting ball of fury who ran up the slope with the energy of a man who had been denied what was his.

'I'll kill you,' he shouted. 'You will all die unless you surrender. You have served your purpose and you are no longer needed!' This was not quite true, for although they had dug out a great deal of the gold there was still much left. On the other hand, if he went now then he still had millions of dollars worth of the precious substance.

Men fell to either side of him but he seemed to have the miraculous ability to dodge bullets, or perhaps it was the fact that he was presenting a moving target. Enough of his men were getting through to the point when they would be able to slaughter the ringleaders of what he saw as a rebellion by the villagers, and he'd gather those who were left and make them work in the mines. A thin smile tightened his lips as he advanced and looked forward to killing those who were getting in his way.

Ramirez moved forward slowly, holding his rifle to the fore, trying to manoeuvre into a position from which he could shoot more directly and kill at least one of the snipers. Despite the roaring of the troopers running up the hills he was able to hear a sound behind him.

He turned round and for a moment, influenced by his

early upbringing, he wanted to make the sign of the cross followed the words *santo le madre de dios*, for there was a ghostly figure in white with long shimmering hair coming towards him, seeming to float above the uneven ground towards him, but it was the girl whom Rivero had been meaning to deflower.

His hesitation cost him his life, for there had been a plentiful supply of weapons left in the camp. She lifted a slender arm and fired a shot from a handgun straight at him. The shot took him in the forehead before he could even raise his rifle, and his face took on an expression of surprise more than anything as the bullet felled him. He pitched forward on to his face and the girl just stood there, an almost dreamy look on her face, and let the gun fall to the ground.

It was the opportunity that Clay, who had been hiding in the rocks forward of where Ramirez was shot, had been waiting for. He emerged holding his rifle, ignoring the girl for the moment, and ran around the building to where his companions were being held back. It was a good example of how troopers who had been trained in a certain degree of response were not able to cope with changing circumstances. He appeared and felled two of them before they were able to respond, while the two hidden snipers, Holt and Flynn, were able to take out the third man by working together. Holt ran up to the girl.

'Get back into the fort until it's over,' he said.

'I killed him,' she said.

'You saved us,' said Holt, 'now save yourself.' He hurried after his friends who were running after the makeshift army.

*

Back in the trees with his father, Ryan had come forward, leaving his father alone but with a gun in his hand. He knew how desperate the situation was. Bert, Aimee and one or two of the villagers were armed with guns they had taken from the dead troops, Scott and Mack had their handguns, while Ryan had his rifle and a Colt shoved into his belt. Then he was aware that there was a figure by his side. It was Hawk and he was walking slowly, grimly, with the determination of a man who was not going to miss out on what he had started. Ryan gave his father a startled look but he did not say anything. They both knew why he was there.

'Get amongst the trees behind me,' said Hawk to the villagers. 'Some of you might be able to escape in the country around us. Don't make it easy for them and don't stay together.' They were already running before he finished his words, some of them having already hidden from the so-called troops a while ago. The pass through which they had arrived in this place was one of the places to which they were heading, but it was some distance away. Hawk and those who stood with him did not pay much attention to what was going on as the troops charged over the hill, led by Rivero. Hawk was abruptly face to face with the man who had caused so much disgrace and destruction to the people of Hatton Falls.

Rivero was a leader who knew another of the same type. He headed straight for Hawk as he came over the slope, a hideous smile on his narrow features. Then he and his men crouched and aimed down at the slope behind the bluff where the people of the village faced them, all bearing their own weapons. More than twenty of the troopers had survived, and they were not men who were about to show mercy to those who were on the verge of destroying their plans to acquire large amounts of gold. In a short time the rancher rebels would be dead and the remaining slaves could go back to their work.

Except there was a collective shout from the pass through which Hawk and his companions had arrived, and a seemingly endless stream of armed men came through bearing a variety of guns and rifles that more than matched that of the enemy. They were led by a somewhat disgruntled-looking Frank Lamington, who had a wild look in his eyes. The added bodies quickly took note of what was happening and ran forward to join Hawk and his companions, and they were all armed and ready to fire. The bandits were not stupid; they knew that they were now the ones facing death or imprisonment. Some were defiant and stayed where they were, but others broke ranks and fled, because as far as they were concerned they were not going to die for the sake of Rivero and his lost cause.

Yancey, who had been standing there like a force of nature ready to be unleashed, leapt forward and chased after them, yelling the whole time and terrifying the fleeing men.

Hawk was the closest to the front and now he ran forward, shouting 'Rivero! Coward!' at the retreating backs. Rivero, who had been running with the rest, turned and pointed a handgun straight at Hawk.

'Die, usurper,' he yelled, but it was the moment Hawk had been waiting for and he had not wanted to shoot a man in the back. He raised his own gun and shot Rivero straight through the heart. The leader of the secret army gave a scream that was more one of rage than pain and kept his gun raised by a supreme effort of will. He began to squeeze the trigger but he need not have bothered, because Hawk pitched forward on his face even as Rivero fell backwards. The Mexican tyrant was as dead as the rocky surface on which he lay.

CHAPTER TWENTY-ONE

Later on, the prisoners were enclosed behind what remained of the enclosure, where the gates had remained secure. The wall on the far side was the one that had remained whole, so ironically the place where the villagers had been held was the one area where the bandits could be kept. Some of them had chosen to fight to the end rather than be taken prisoner, running into the bullets of Holt, Clay and Flynn. That still meant about seventeen of the original raiders had been taken, some of them from a hunting party that had not taken part in the actual fighting.

Hawk lay in the bed that had once been occupied by Rivero, and it was plain that he was far from well. By his side were his men, who looked more than exhausted, needing rest after their privations but determined to see that their boss – and friend – was going to survive. Beside them were his son Ryan, and Abbey, the girl who had stayed by his side, with whom he had defied the guards and whom he had taken a beating for – but they had left her alone after that.

'Where's Lena?' asked Abbey, but in a tone of concern rather than jealousy.

'She's being looked after by Aimee, and so is Bert,' said Ryan. 'They're both doing well, and I have a feeling Aimee is going to look after them both a lot more in that boarding house of hers.'

The man in the bed lay there, looking as if he were already dead as Scott McArthur and Mack Jardine entered the room.

'Get out,' said Ryan shortly, but Scott gave a nervous look at the man lying beneath the blankets.

'I know it ain't going to convince you,' he said, 'but he's my uncle and you're my cousin. What I did was mighty stupid, and I guess I'm asking you for a chance.' He looked down and scuffed his feet, and suddenly Ryan had a picture of the young boy he had known. 'I was going to stick around for the gold, was going to cheat and lie and get it and ride off, but what's the point? I ain't ambitious and neither's Mack; we would waste any money we had in a month and be back to square one. Give us a chance.'

'No,' said Abbey, 'they won't change. Don't listen to them.'

Scott looked her squarely in the face, only his flickering eyelids showing how nervous he was. 'I guess I did real bad by you, Abbey. It was greed and it was chance. I'll make it up if I ever can.'

'It's up to you, Ryan,' said Abbey.

'No, it's up to me,' said a sepulchral voice. They all turned to the bed. For the first time since pitching over, Hawk was opening his eyes. He turned his head and groaned a little at the pain in his body.

'Dad!' Ryan flew across the room to his father's side. Hawk struggled and with the help of his son managed to half-sit against the pine headboard. Hawk took a drink of water and seemed to gasp for a while, but then he seemed better.

'We're family,' he said, 'every single one of us around this bed. I'm not following your mother, Ryan, I'm staying here and so are these young men. We'll keep a watch on them, but Ryan, I could see with my own eyes: Scott saved your life, and Mack is just not that strong a boy in the head. If your cousin wants to work, we'll work him. It'll be hard, but if he's telling the truth, we'll help him.' He paused and looked around those who were still in his life. 'We've turned from revenge riders to what we were: ranchers, and those cows need tending.' He coughed again. 'Sleep'll do me good, and we'll build the kind of ranch your mother would have wanted. Abbey, you're welcome if you can put up with all these men, but we'll have female housekeepers, too, and you can see the girls in the village any time you want.'

The girl looked thoughtful. She looked at Scott and he had the grace to look ashamed, while Holt, Flynn and Clay looked paternal.

'All these big men to look after me?' she asked. 'And I won't be the only woman when these guys get married – they've all got sweethearts, I'm sure – and there's always the village, and plenty of work. What have I got in

159

Houston? Slavery and drudgery from my aunt ... She hated me, you know, because I was young and pretty. I'll do it.'

'Good,' said Hawk. 'Now all of you get out.'

'Are you OK?' asked Ryan anxiously.

'Damn right I am,' said Hawk. 'This is the first real bed I've been in for a long time. I'm going to snuggle down, sleep for a day, then get to work with the rest of you.'

They left, knowing there was a long hard road ahead for all of them, yet in the back of their minds was the gold dug out so laboriously by the villagers. The district was going to be rich. Hatton Falls was going to be prosperous and they all knew Hawk of the hills would make sure the money went to the right places. And people.